The Candidate:

Memoirs of a Centaur

Also by Mario Milosevic

Novels
Claypot Dreamstance
The Coma Monologues
The Doctor and the Clown
Kyle's War
The Last Giant
Splitting
Terrastina and Mazolli: a Novel in 99-Word Chapters

Collections
15 Strange Tales of Crime and Mystery
A Bestiary of Imaginary Species
Entangled Realites (with Kim Antieau)
Labor Days
Miniatures
Mostly Invisble

Poetry
Alien Life
Animal Life
Bugs!
Fantasy Life
Love Life
Mario Writes a Poem a Day for A Year and So Can You

Nonfiction
The First 500 Primes Written Out in Alphabetical Order
Kim and Mario Build a Labyrinth and So Can You (with Kim Antieau)

MARIO MILOSEVIC

THE CANDIDATE
Memoirs of a Centaur

The Candidate: Memoirs of a Centaur
by Mario Milosevic
Copyright ©2025 by Mario Milosevic

Published by Up All Night Books,
an imprint of Green Snake Publishing
www.greensnakepublishing.com

ISBN: 978-1-949644-74-6

This book is a wholly artisanal work of creation by the author, a sentient being. It was written without any input from artificial intelligence.

Thanks to Nancy Milosevic

Cover image by tongdang | depositphotos
Centaur silhouette image by Krisdog | depositphotos
Logo image by wordspotrayal | depositphotos.com

ONE

The worst part, by far, is that I'm the only one of my kind.

As far as I know. Now, there could be another centaur on the planet. I suppose it's possible. But I haven't found one yet, and neither has anyone else, so the reasonable assumption is that I'm it.

People and horses, both species are social creatures. Put us together into one organism, like what happened with me, and one of two things could then occur. First, the horse and human aspects could cancel each other out and you'd end up with a solitary creature happy in his solitude.

Or two, you could end up with someone who wants to run with other centaurs and spend time with other centaurs. You'd have someone who likes to maybe joins clubs where he passes pleasant evenings in the company of other centaurs, perhaps playing games or discussing books. Or maybe you get a centaur who just wants to go to movies with other centaurs. Someone who wants to date other centaurs. That sort of thing.

In other words, you'd end up with me.

I'm that lonely centaur who yearns to talk to other centaurs about life as a myth made manifest in 21st century America.

Instead, I'm going to use the medium of memoir to tell the world about me.

Not that the world cares.

They used to. Back when I appeared from God only knows where, I was more than a curiosity. I was an instant celebrity.

I fell out of the sky. Ended up with a broken leg. If I hadn't had a human torso, arms, and head, I would probably have been shot since that's what you do with horses that have broken legs. Don't think I haven't thought about that. The privilege that humans accrue upon themselves, simply by being human, is something most humans are completely blind to.

Anyway. There I was, a rainy November on the Oregon side of the Columbia River Gorge, my hide getting soaked, me trying to gain some foothold on the mud and gravel under me, but I was flopped on one side, and the pain was

A precarious perch  7

shooting up through my damaged leg, my right rear leg, into my brain.

I could raise my head and torso, but the effort was not one I could sustain for long and I ended up using my arms to try to keep myself up off the ground and not really succeeding. I was also in a precarious position.

To one side, far down a sheer cliff, a creek, flowing swift over jutting boulders, showed white foam and broadcast a constant sound of water hissing over rocks. It felt like it was trying to tell me something, but I didn't know the language.

On the other side, an edifice of moss-covered rock going straight up to a misty clump of damp air. I was sprawled on a hiking path between those two extremes, and my legs were kicking at the mud, sending up sprays of it, while I called out in pain.

Many times since that morning I've wondered why I was there. I don't remember anything before that moment. Was I constructed in the sky as I fell? Was I the spawn of some evil scientist's laboratory? Did I emerge from the rocks, like some ghost rising out of the Earth? Did the myth-makers of the world find some source of power that allowed their demented thought creations to manifest in the real world?

I don't know. And no one who has studied me since has any idea either. Best anyone can come up with is that I was—am—some kind of strange anomaly that only comes along once in a lifetime. Or once an era.

8 A perilous predicament

You can't begin to fathom the loneliness encompassed by that sentence.

But I digress.

Let me get back to that singularly dreary day. It was the day of my creation, but it did not resemble a joyous birth. Instead, it was some kind of cruel cosmic joke. I had four powerful legs. I had the strength of a horse. By rights I should have been galloping across the countryside, feeling the wind in my face and the sheer joy of flight.

Instead, I was perched precariously over the edge of a cliff. I felt myself slipping, the weight of my back end pulling me down.

As I raised myself up to take a look at my injury, I saw that the bone was definitely broken. The leg was flopped at an odd angle. No way was I going to stand on that leg. Nope.

But beyond the injured leg: open air above the creek. If I wasn't especially careful, I was going to slip over the edge of the trail.

If I fell to what looked like the bottom of a hundred foot drop to the creek below, I was not going to survive. My head would most likely be smashed against the rocks on the side, and if I did make it to the water below, I would probably be swept away on the current and drown.

Over the ensuing decades, I've thought about that moment. Often. Letting go might have been the most merciful thing I could have done for myself. Dying, only moments after birth, had a certain poetry to it. I would have been a strange corpse washed downstream where curious hikers would have found me and reported me and I would have been the source of endless speculation.

Probably been the sort of thing that Bigfoot hunters would have seized on. See, they might have said, we told you there were strange things in the Pacific Northwest. See? See?

But that didn't happen. The instinct for survival was strong in me, a curse, you might say. The sort of thing that overrides everything else, even common sense.

I grabbed at tree branches hanging low enough to help me. I kicked with my good legs, finding purchase even with clumsy hooves as leverage, and managed to pull myself up and over the lip of the edge of the trail and lay there in a massive puddle. The rain drops sent up little splashy geysers all around me in constantly changing constellations of waterspouts.

I was hungry. That was the overriding feeling I had. I wanted to eat something. Anything. Although, deep in the back of my mind, there was a hankering for, of all things, hay.

Really? I asked myself if that was truly what I wanted.

It appeared so.

As I was thus engaged, thinking about what I might eat, and trying to find a way to get ambulatory, despite my broken leg, I heard voices behind me.

I twisted around and saw two hikers.

10   I am embarrassed

They were stopped on the trail. Staring at me. And why wouldn't they?

They were two women, each wearing rain coats, one bright yellow, the other purple. They also bore walking sticks, knapsacks, and the widest eyes I think I have ever seen. I must have presented quite a sight.

I used my good legs to dig into the mud and I spun myself around so that I was facing them. I was hungry and cold. I had no clothes on, and I felt like my modesty was not well served by the fur covering my lower body. I was acutely aware of my junk, since it was not covered, and my broken leg prevented me from modestly covering that area. I believe I turned red. I must have looked like I was overheating, even though I was shivering from the cold and the rain. Not to mention the shock of being there.

"Help me," I said, regretting that my first words were pitiful. It would have been so much better to have been able to say something powerful.

I listened to rain spattering against their waterproof hats. Watched as their brains must have done some quick thinking, perhaps calculating.

One of them licked her lips. "What are you?"

"I don't know," I said. And I didn't. Not then. I was a being in trouble, but that wasn't an identity. It was a condition.

They looked at each other, then back at me. "What's wrong with you?"

"Broken leg," I said.

A reassuring touch 

"Who should I call?" asked one of them.

I didn't have time to answer. The other one came over and put her hand on my flank. She looked into my eyes. I looked back. I saw fear, certainly, but some semblance of caring and empathy as well. She was a brave person to approach someone such as myself, who she could only have known from books or movies or strange dreams. She could not have had any kind of actual contact with anyone remotely like me.

The contact was more than welcome. Her hand was warm and reassuring. I did notice she kept to my horse aspect, smoothing the fur and keeping away from my human aspect. Too unsettling, perhaps?

Her caring strokes were the assurance I needed that I was not alone. That I was a being worthy of compassion.

I didn't then know how ridiculous that thought was.

TWO

Transporting me out of the trail was no easy task. The stretchers that Search and Rescue use to get injured people to civilization and safety were obviously inadequate for my case.

More hikers joined the first two. No one kept walking past me. I was, apparently, too interesting to ignore.

They called for a tractor and wagon. I was struck by the bravery of whoever it was who chose to assist me. The trail, as I mentioned, was narrow and slippery. The vehicle

12   I ask for help

would take a good hour to maneuver the mile or so from the trailhead to my position on it.

In the meantime the gathering hikers tried to reassure me that everything was going to be okay. I complained about the pain in my leg and told them over and over how hungry I was.

Rescuers from Search and Rescue arrived ahead of the tractor. They handed me energy bars. Tiny things. I ate them. They felt like they descended into a cavernous space, my stomach. I discerned immediately that my life was going to be a torment of trying to feed and nourish a horse's body through a human's mouth. The mismatch was a curse. I would have to eat constantly.

People took pictures of me on their cell phones. Then, presumably, they posted them to their social media sites. A few of the S & R folks tried to stop them, but that was a completely futile effort. More hikers came down the trail and stopped.

At one point someone tried to put a blanket over my human part. I grabbed it and tossed it to the creek below.

"Whoa, dude," he said. "Just trying to give you some privacy."

"Forget privacy," I said in what I can only describe as a snarl. "Get me out of here. Get me to someone who can help me."

"I can help you," he said. "I'll put a bullet through your head." He made a gun shape with his thumb and forefinger and jerked it up and down. "Pop pop pop," he said. "Just like that, man."

Others in the group looked at him like he was proposing a meal of baked kittens. He then looked suitably chagrined and shrugged his shoulders.

"Sorry, man," he said. "It's just that, you know, when a horse breaks its leg . . ."

"I know," I said, "but I'm half man."

"Whatever," he said, then retreated down the trail a little, making a pretense of looking for the tractor. "Where *is* that thing," he asked the air.

I turned from him and looked straight at a hiker with a camera.

"Let me see one of those shots," I said.

The hiker shook her head. "You're going to break my camera," she said.

"I will not." I reached for her, digging my front hooves into the ground, then gaining purchase against the cliff and moving closer to her. "I want to know what I look like," I said with a grimace, barely getting the words out because the pain of my broken leg was overwhelming.

She stepped back.

"Give it to me!" I said.

She froze, then extended her arm toward me and I grabbed the camera and turned it around and looked at the images she had taken.

I didn't know what to expect. How could I? The preview screen showed a not very handsome man attached to

14   I am offered a coat

the body of a horse. I had something of a pot belly, which protruded way more than I was comfortable with. My head was mostly bald, with some remnants of dark brown hair arcing over my ears. My chest sagged, my arms were flabby, and I had a beard that badly needed trimming. I looked like an out-of-shape mountain man.

My horse half, on the other hand, was sleek and strong. I could see muscles bulging along my sides and over my back. My tail was lushly brown, and the color of my fur faded a little toward my hooves, like it had been designed that way. Gave me a smart kind of look, like someone cared about my appearance and wanted to make me as presentable as possible.

I remember feeling shame. A lot of it. My hands trembled and my head felt hot. I expected my human half to be much better looking. What was the point of being a centaur if I couldn't be handsome?

I gave the camera back to the hiker. She took it, gingerly, but she no longer seemed afraid of me. That was okay, I suppose, but also a little deflating. I wanted to be powerful. Wanted to be at least a little bit intimidating.

I asked the other guy for the blanket again. I suddenly wanted to cover myself.

He laughed at me. I didn't get the joke.

Someone else, another good samaritan, overcome by my predicament, offered his coat. I took it and put it on, gritting teeth the whole time. The pain was still there. Sharp and shooting.

People let me drink from their water bottles. I got everyone's germs. I didn't care, but it wasn't enough. I needed a lot of water.

A man who, I surmised, was in charge of the operation patted me on the shoulder. As I was leaning over at the time, with my side in the mud, it was a strangely un-reassuring gesture. I much preferred contact on my horse region, where the fur was, well, more—*nice*—would be the best word. Contact on my human portion was invasive and unpleasant. Like clammy hands were trying to find a kinship with me when I felt no kinship with anything.

Did I mention I was alone in the world?

We heard the whine of a tractor some distance away. The man in charge asked me my name.

"I don't know," I said.

"You don't know your own name?"

I shook my head.

"You got some kind of amnesia?"

"I don't know," I said. "I feel like I have working knowledge of things on this world. I'm going to be taken to a hospital, I assume. Or a vet's office. I have a picture of such things in my head. I know there are cars and buildings and people who do things. I know about elections and schools. I understand institutions like restaurants and museums. I know the world is a globe, that there are cities and farms and coastlines and ships that cross oceans. It's all in there." I tapped my temple.

"But not your name."

 # A name I like

I shook my head again.

"You want us to give you one?"

"What's yours?" I asked.

"Melville," he said.

"Not a very good name," I said. "Makes me think of something from another century. I'm not sure you should be naming me."

He laughed. "You're a funny guy," he said. "My parents named me. Not me."

"But you kept it," I said.

"That's how things are."

I thought about it and realized he was right.

"So you're saying someone else should name me."

He nodded. "Traditionally it's your parents, but I have a hunch you don't know where they are."

I nodded. "True."

"You remember them?"

"No."

"So you don't know if one of them was a horse and other was human."

"I don't know how I got here," I said, "but I'm pretty sure that's not the way it works. Can't work, actually."

He looked puzzled for a second, then he stood up and addressed the group gathered around me.

"He wants a name," he said. "He wants us to name him."

That wasn't exactly true, but I let it go.

My injury worsens  17

Suggestions came fast and furious. "Tex." "Baldy." "Trigger." "Lightning." "Flabby."

I lay in silent humiliation until one of the women who first saw me suggested "Cal."

I liked it immediately. "Yes," I said. "I'll be Cal."

She beamed. I smiled back at her.

It was a moment. Sweet and lovely. I had an identity. I was happy.

The tractor turned a corner. Everyone cheered. Including me.

It chugged toward us, towing a trailer. A long trailer that I surmised I was supposed to get into.

That's when someone looked down at my broken leg and pointed in alarm.

"Shit," he said. "The guy's bleeding. A lot."

THREE

Somehow the end of my break had torn through my skin. The jagged white bone was prominent in the dark air that surrounded us all.

From the wound a steady flow of blood was spilling onto the trail, staining a puddle deep red.

I don't know how I had not noticed that up until then. Probably happened when I was twisting myself around to get a look at the camera.

Melville tore off the scarf he had around his neck and cinched it around the upper thigh of my broken leg.

18   In an altered state

I felt faint from the mere sight of the blood coursing down my leg. By this time the tractor was close. The driver stopped her vehicle and jumped out and ran over to me. She had a first aid kit. She bent over my leg.

"My name is Allison," she said. "I'm a vet."

Melville stepped aside.

"I'm Cal," I said.

"Nice to meet you," she said. "I didn't believe them when they said I was going to be treating a centaur."

"Joke's on you, then," I said.

"Looks that way. This is a nasty break."

"I can't argue with you," I said.

She maneuvered herself around the wound so she was between me and the blood. I was grateful for that, but also a little disturbed by it. Was my wound so awful that she didn't want me to see it?

"You're going to feel a little pain," she said.

"I already do," I said. "But it's okay. Me and pain, we've been companions all my life. All my short life. We respect each other."

"Uh huh," she said, and then I did feel a sharp pain where she stuck a needle into me.

"Oh," I said. "That's a strange feeling."

A wave of euphoria came over me. I suddenly felt like the world was a wonderful place. The rain was so pleasant and refreshing. I put out my hand to catch some of the drops.

"He's gone loopy," said Melville.

"It's a powerful painkiller," said Allison. "I always figured it did things to horses, but none of them ever talked back to me. Now one does."

"Red letter day all around," said Melville.

This struck me as so funny that I had to laugh. Which I did. Loudly and at great length.

"How you propose to get him onto that trailer?" asked Melville.

"I brought a tarp," said Allison. "It's in the trailer."

A tarp. She had the foresight to bring a tarp. Again, the humor of the moment was not lost on me. I began giggling. It was actually a little bit embarrassing.

Allison got back into her kit and pulled out a bottle of antiseptic and poured it over my wound. Then she retrieved a needle and thread and began sewing up my wound. She whistled as she worked. My vision was getting fuzzy and the world seemed like a distant thing, all gauzy and soft, like a picture out of focus.

Melville went away and then came back with a large plastic sheet. The plastic looked thick and strong. He put it down on the ground next to me and asked Allison if she was done.

"Almost," she said. "Get me a strong stick. Two feet long. Couple of inches in diameter."

"Okay," said Melville. He looked at me and smiled. "You're getting the finest care available," he said.

"Glad to hear it," I said. My voice was so distant, it felt like I was listening to something at the bottom of a well. I

20   Quick to take offense

tried to reach into the well and retrieve my words. I had a notion to pull on their ends and make them bigger so more people could see them. It felt particularly important, at that moment, for my words to fill the world.

Someone handed Melville a branch that matched Allison's request. He took it and handed it to Allison who then put it against my leg and secured it in place with tape from her kit. It was a crude splint, but would have to do under the circumstances.

Allison stood up and slapped her palms one against the other. "Done!" she said.

"Good," said Melville. "Now let's get him onto this tarp. Cal, you up to helping us?"

"I'm disabled," I said. "I need help, not the other way around. Why don't you get that?"

"I get it," said Melville, "but you're a big guy."

"Not my fault."

"Just get yourself moved onto the tarp."

I didn't care for his attitude. A bit rude. I told him as much. He didn't seem to care.

"The tarp," he said. "Come on Cal. Giddy-up."

I twisted my human part around so I was staring Melville in the face. We weren't separated by more than a foot. His eyes were wary, and mine, I'm sure, were blazing.

"Don't tell me to giddy-up," I said.

He put up his hands, palms toward me, and tilted his head to the side in a show of surrender. Or some kind of mock friendliness, I couldn't be sure which.

"Didn't mean to offend," he said.

I turned from him, twisting myself back, and used my good legs to brace myself on the rock face and push myself onto the tarp.

It was big enough to hold me.

Then the people who were all still there, still amused or fascinated by the centaur in trouble, they all surged forward and grabbed the edge of the tarp. I believe there were about twenty of them.

"Easy," said Allison. She patrolled the area near my broken leg as I was lifted off the ground with the tarp and moved the few feet to the trailer behind the tractor.

They worked as gently as they could and I kept myself from kicking, though the instinct was there and it took a lot of effort to keep myself from doing so.

As I settled onto the trailer bed, the edges of it bit into my skin and pinched my fur. It was also cold against my belly, which stuck out from under the jacket I was wearing.

There was no good place for my head. I rested it against the side, but it was hard metal, and it hurt my neck.

"I could use a pillow," I said to no one in particular.

Before long someone pushed a rolled up knapsack under my head. It offered some comfort, but not much. I thought to complain about this, but did not want to get a reputation and determined that I would put up with the discomfort. What else could I do?

Just about everyone that had had a hand in holding the tarp took their turn patting my flank.

22   The possibility of a fall

The first few were kind of nice, then it became annoying.

Again, no complaints from me. I just gritted my teeth and tolerated the invasion of my privacy. They all thought they could violate my personal space just because they had offered me some assistance. I struggled, with little success, to understand this point of view.

They unhooked the tractor and moved it around and hooked it to the hitch on the other end of the trailer.

Allison got into the seat of the tractor and started it and we got going.

Cheers from the assembled people.

I wanted to talk to Allison, but I was situated so my human portion was at the trailing end. She glanced back at me, and said something. I couldn't tell what it was. I was still up in the sky, feeling the effects of the painkiller she had given me.

The trail had some wicked curves, and spots where the trail narrowed to a width hardly more than the distance between the tractor's tires. I watched as the ground rolled under me.

The trailer also skidded a few times. I called to Allison over the sound of the tractor. I tried to tell her to slow down.

But we were going down. The tractor was a little hard to control, it seemed. We slipped more than once.

I saw the creek, still there pushing water along next to the trail. Shadowing it.

Inevitably, I suppose, my precarious situation only got worse.

The trailer, fishtailing behind the tractor, went too far to one side, and hit the cliff wall, then bounced off of it and skidded across the trail and one of the wheels went over the side far enough that the edge of the drop-off caught the bottom of the trailer and held it fast.

The tractor, still trying to keep going, got batted across the trail as well, and ended up, like the trailer, half hanging over the edge.

Allison cried out.

I cried out.

Below me, the creek was not as far down as it was where I first landed, but it was far enough. Falling would cause serious injury.

Allison jumped out of the tractor and ran around to the end of the trailer.

The trailer, it seemed, was not interested in remaining in place for her convenience.

It slipped even further over the edge and my stomach felt like the world had dropped out from under it and the wash of water over rocks suddenly became the most menacing sound in the world.

FOUR

Gradually the sound of the water over the rocks was replaced with a drumbeat sound that I didn't at first recog-

24   Allison fights for me

nize. It bothered me that I couldn't place the sound, because it was the kind of sound that overtakes everything.

The air got beaten by the noise. Allison, I suppose not knowing what else to do, grabbed the edge of the trailer and yelled at me to get off. I tried to shift my weight so that it wasn't helping to slide the trailer over the edge, but that wasn't working. Whatever I did, the trailer kept slipping.

I was hoping it was going to catch on the axle and stop the sliding, but I didn't know if that was going to happen.

Then Allison looked up at the sky. I felt wind pushing down on me and followed Allison's gaze to see, hovering above me, a helicopter and a man on the end of a line, coming down.

He touched ground beside the trailer and nodded at first to Allison, then me.

"I'm taking over," he said.

"This is my patient," said Allison.

"Ma'am," he said, "it wasn't an invitation for a discussion. I'm taking over."

"I want Allison to be involved," I said.

He pointed at me. "No talking," he said. I saw a distinct look of distaste on his face, like he had put something in his mouth he was now pretty sure was rotten.

I didn't like his attitude.

"What authority do you have to tell me what to do?" I asked.

"By the authority that I'm going to save your fucked up life."

The end of the rope he came down on had six hooks. I noticed the tarp that Allison and the others had used to put me in the trailer had six rings along the edge.

He began to put the hooks into the rings. Allison stepped forward to help. I even reached out for one of the hooks, but he didn't allow it.

"Step back," he said to Allison, with an authority that seemed to indicate he was not usually contradicted.

He did the rest of the hooks, then signaled to the pilot in the helicopter above us to lift me and the tarp.

I felt myself rise above the trailer, and slowly cleared it. A second later the trailer and the tractor both went over the edge and fell to the creek below, breaking on the way down.

I felt elation that I had narrowly escaped that fate.

The tarp was wrapped tightly around me. It was playing hell with my broken leg. The pain was enough that I felt as though I was about to black out. I fought to keep myself awake.

I was able to wrestle my head and arms around so that I could hang over the edge of the tarp and look down. Allison and the man were both still on the trail, staring up at me. Allison waved. I waved back.

Then the helicopter increased altitude and speed. It still beat the air with an intensity I didn't much care for. It was hurting my ears. I put my hands over them, but the beating went right through me. I felt it in my bones, especially my broken bone.

26   Deposited onto a table

I looked down. We flew over the Columbia River, though I didn't know that's what it was called, not at that time. The river was a wide meandering expanse that crawled through green forest and high cliffs. I saw waterfalls on both sides of the gorge, lovely threads of white and blue marking the rocks.

A dam cut the river in one place. I saw cascading white water on one side of the dam, sailboarders crisscrossing the water on the other.

A ship hauling wood chips rode the current toward Portland. We were going in the opposite direction.

I don't know how long I was in the air. I probably passed out a few times. I felt groggy and violated.

As we continued east, the rain got less and less intense until it disappeared completely. The sun didn't come out, but I was no longer being pelted by raindrops. A cover of clouds kept the blue sky away from view.

The landscape below me went from lush green forest to a dry brown scrubland: Grass and a few scraggly trees.

We veered off the path of the river, north over a patchwork quilt of various squares of different shades of green, which I guessed was irrigated crop fields.

Finally, we came to a small grouping of tents, five in all. They were white and fluttered in a brisk breeze.

As we slowly descended to a spot near these tents, several people in white coats came running out of the tents. A few of them pushed an enormous table on wheels. It stopped below me, and that is where the helicopter pilot who I was never to meet, deposited me.

The tarp relaxed against my sides.

Several faces, covered in surgical masks, stared at me.

I heard voices.

"It's real," said one.

"I'm still not sure I believe it," said another.

"Believe what you see," said the first.

They pushed the table, with me flopped on my side, tired and dirty, rattling on top of it. I got another shot in my rear end. No one asked me if I wanted it. I did not have time to protest.

As I went under, I heard voices, watery and distant, but also they felt like they were right there next to me. Almost inside my head.

"We'll take care of the leg, of course, then we'll do the other thing."

"Yeah. Important to do the other thing. For everyone's sake, even though he won't like it."

What wasn't I going to like? What were they thinking of doing to me?

I fought the sedative. I called out for Allison. I told them, as loudly as I could, that I wanted Allison. She understood me. She wanted to help me.

But my words were too faint, and, in any case, they weren't interested in anything I had to say.

FIVE

Time passed, though I was unaware of it. I had dreams. My two parts had been separated and I walked as both a man and a horse.

There was freedom and sadness as a consequence. In my human aspect I met a female and we coupled.

In my equine aspect I was presented with females in estrus and bred with them.

The dreams were not pleasant ones at all. There was a blanket of melancholy over everything and none of the couplings, human or equine, resulted in any offspring, which tore at my heart.

When I awoke, I was on my side. The room was dark. Several people were clustered around me.

"He's coming out of it," said a woman in a white lab coat. Was it Allison? I looked at her carefully. My vision was blurry and I felt crusty crumbles on my eyelashes. I worked my fists into the sockets to clear my vision.

Not Allison.

I sighed, and felt pain in my chest. I would have to call it heartache.

Someone else, also in a white lab coat, stepped forward. "I'm going to examine you now," he said.

I didn't feel any need to stop him. "Fine," I said.

As he put his stethoscope on me, and as I watched a dozen pairs of eyes looking at me, I began to feel as though something was missing. It was a kind of nebulous sensation at first. Something on the edge of my awareness. I wanted to ask someone in the room about it, but gradually it became clear.

I *was* missing something.

I pulled away from the ridiculous man and twisted around to get a view of my horse parts. My leg was impressively wrapped in a cast. The cast was red, which surprised me. I had expected white. I did not feel any pain associated with the leg. Either they had done a good job, or they had me on painkillers. At that moment, I honestly did not now know which it was.

"We looked up your history," said one of the onlookers. He did not wear a lab coat. He was dressed in a suit and tie, completely incongruous with the rest of the entourage attending to me.

"What history?" I asked.

"Seems many of your kind are—aggressive."

"You found others of my kind?" I asked, feeling shame for betraying eagerness.

"No," he said. "I mean, we read about your ancestors."

I blinked. "You mean books?"

"Yes, books. Legends written down. Your earliest relatives were found by the Greeks. Ancient Greeks. There were warlike groups of you. You raided villages. You were good with bows. Your arrows went straight and true. You carried off women."

30   My new circumstances

I was getting a headache just listening to him. Did I need a lesson in mythology? "Get to the point," I said.

"The point is, we did a surgery on you."

Something about his tone in that sentence broke my ignorance. I suddenly knew exactly what he referred to. I lifted my broken leg and looked at the area and saw that, indeed, the good people who had rescued me from the muddy trail had also taken it upon themselves to improve me. I was now a gelding.

I must have turned red. I felt my face get hot and my hands shook with—what? Rage? Sadness? I wasn't sure.

"It was for your own good," said the suit. "And for ours. We intend, in good time, to release you to the world, but it could not happen with you in a whole state. I'm sure you understand."

Of course I did not understand.

"You had no right," I said.

"Perhaps not, but we had the wisdom and the means."

"I'm not dangerous."

"That has yet to be determined."

I pushed away the guy with the stethoscope, employing rather more force than was necessary.

He put his hands out as he lost his balance and almost fell on his ass, saved only by the swift and sure intervention of some of his compatriots, who caught him and raised him back to his feet.

"I see what you mean," he said to the room with a smirk on his face, which I took an instant disliking to.

My abuse continues  31

"I want a lawyer," I said.

They all looked puzzled. "You don't need a lawyer," said one of them. "We are looking after all your needs. You have a dedicated team of responsible individuals who have only your best interests at heart."

Here rage asserted itself strongly in me. I determined that I was going to get them. I twisted my body around on the table until my rear end pointed in their direction and kicked with my good leg as hard as I could.

I was surprised by my speed and agility. I was not at all sure that I had it in me to do what I had just done.

I connected.

My hoof caught one of them in the side. She went down, holding her hand up, as though she might be able to grab something that would lift her off her feet.

Nothing was there, and my action proved to be a mistake, for at that moment three burly guys approached me and surrounded me. I kicked again, but they were strategically placed so I did not connect again. The rest of the group retreated and pressed their backs against the wall while the three burly guys grabbed me by the arms and held me while someone else approached with a needle.

"Don't stick me," I said. "Don't do it. You have no right. *You have no right!*"

But such statements did nothing for my well-being because one of the burly guys hit me across the mouth, which stunned me. I felt blood trickle down my chin.

The guy with the needle was just about to make contact

32 I am offered a rescue

with my hindquarter when the door burst open and several people wearing ski masks, sporting assault rifles, and wearing black clothes, came pouring into the room.

They pointed their weapons at the rest of the people in the room. The guy with the needle put up his hands and dropped the needle.

The burly dudes released me.

"Get some clothes on," said one of the invaders. "You're about to be rescued."

SIX

I was baffled as to why they needed me clothed, but as I began searching frantically for a shirt or a jacket or *something*, they had herded all the other people, the ones who had been responsible for my now neutered condition, into a small adjoining room and pushed a heavy desk against it.

I didn't think that was going to hold them, at least not for long, but I didn't say anything.

"I don't have a shirt," I said.

"Never mind," said one of the gun toters. A female voice. She handed me a bow and an arrow.

I did not have the wits to refuse her. I took the weapons, then held them like they were pieces of wood I had found on the forest floor.

She must have noticed my puzzlement.

"You're a centaur."

"Yes. So?"

"Centaurs are good archers."

"Who told you that?"

"No one told me. Everyone knows it."

Two others came close to her and one of them whispered in her ear.

Meanwhile the captives in the adjoining room were getting restless. They banged on the door.

One of the invaders swung his weapon around, yelled "Shut up!" and put several bullets in the space above the door. "The next ones will be about five feet lower," he said.

Silence from the other side of the door.

"Okay," said the woman who had given me the bow. "We don't have a lot of time. Let's get going. Can you walk?"

I threw down first the bow, which clattered on the floor, then the arrows.

"I have a broken leg," I said.

"We know that."

I spread my hands.

"You've got 75 percent mobility. Let's get going."

I folded my arms over my chest.

"Why should I?"

She pointed to the space between my rear legs. "We wouldn't have done that."

"What's done is done. The people here are trying to take care of me. In, I admit, a clumsy and inhumane manner. Also inequine. But they've already done what they're going to do. They feed me and keep me warm. I don't know anything about you."

"Are you serious? You *want* to stay here as an experimental subject? You have no idea what they have planned for you."

"And you do?"

Quiet in the room. I heard voices from behind ski masks. Hard to tell who was talking. "This is fucked up, man." "We should be *gone* by now." "What's with this guy?"

The woman pulled off her ski mask. She had short cropped hair and an intense look in her eyes, like she wanted to attack me. Maybe she did.

"You give up your anonymity and that's supposed to impress me?" I asked. "What's your name?"

"Deb," she said. "I'm Allison's daughter."

The statement was obviously designed to impress me, and it did. But I saw something in her face. A slight twitch. She also looked to the side for an instant. I don't know how I knew this was an indication of lying, but I did know it, viscerally and instinctively.

"I don't believe you," I said.

One of the others, apparently fed up with my reluctance, stepped forward and held his weapon pointed directly as my chest, which, still unclothed, felt particularly vulnerable.

"I've had enough," he said. "We're rescuing you, you dumb ass. Don't fight us."

"You always threaten those you purport to aid?"

With that, the rest of the gang grabbed me by the arm and shoulder and others got behind me and pushed my horse body off the table. I ended up sprawled on the floor. My leg shot pain signals up to my human head, but it wasn't too bad. Nothing I couldn't handle.

They helped me up—I'll give them that—and I stood unsteadily on my three good legs, slipping a little on the floor.

"I'll go with you," I said, "but I'm telling you now, all of you, that it is under protest. I did not ask to be taken away."

"You didn't ask to be brought here, either," said Deb.

"Deb," I said, "if that is your name, which I doubt, it's not up to you to tell me what I should and shouldn't do. It is certainly not up to you to *make* me do anything."

"He's a pain in the ass," said one of her henchmen.

"That he is," said Deb.

We continued walking, me kind of hobbling as I kept my broken leg from touching the ground, which meant I had to kind of hop on the remaining good rear leg.

We soon got outside. The air was cool and there was a wind, which felt quite refreshing for a few seconds, then felt too cold.

"I need a jacket," I said.

"We didn't bring one."

"Not exactly a crackerjack operation you've got going here, is it?"

We approached a large van hooked up to a truck. It was obviously intended for me, as it was tall and big enough to

 ⚔ **Ambiguities of freedom**

accommodate my size. The words ANIMAL LIBERA-TION were printed on the side of the van in big letters.

"What is this?" I asked.

"I told you," said Deb, "we're rescuing you."

"I'm not an animal."

"Half of you is."

"Not the brain part. Not the talking part. Not the part that is in charge of me."

She shrugged. Her minions moved closer to me and grabbed me by the arms and urged me forward. I went, because I couldn't fight them off.

"We're interested in the animal part as much as the human part," she said. "You're one of a kind, as far as anyone knows. As the sole representative of your species, you deserve to be free. Now quit arguing with us and get in the fucking van."

Ah, freedom. It has the power to inspire.

They opened wide doors on the end of the trailer and lowered a ramp that had wooden slabs installed across it for my hooves to gain purchase. I hobbled up the thing, feeling it sag under my weight. I thought it was going to collapse, and I was prepared to tumble to the ground, but that didn't happen.

Once I was inside, they tossed the ramp aside and closed and latched the doors.

Then I heard running footsteps go around me and the engine of the truck start up and we were moving.

"Hey," I said, "I don't have food in here. Or water. I'm

I demand nourishment   37

hungry. I need food." I banged on the end of the trailer with my fist. "Food!" I said. "You are the worst rescuers ever."

I got no answer, and I certainly didn't get any food. I felt my stomach rumbling. Both my stomachs. I had a human one, and an equine one. It felt like a cavernous emptiness. It felt like it could swallow up tons of hay. Yes, hay! I craved hay. I wanted hay. Lots of it. Also carrots. I would have killed for a bunch of carrots.

I was feeling faint and weak. We kept driving. I don't know how long. It could have been hours. Probably was. Maybe days. I beat on the walls several times. We stopped a few places. They finally threw in some water bottles for me, and a few sandwiches.

I wolfed down the food in a few seconds. "More," I said. "I need more."

But they were disgusted with me, and would not get me anything else. I was, apparently, a nuisance.

When we finally stopped, it was in a hot place. The air felt like it was laced with dust and sun rays.

They led me out of the trailer and I walked on desert. Saguaros were arrayed around me.

"So long," said Deb. "And good riddance."

Then all of them, every last one of these so called rescuers, got back in the truck, started the engine and drove off.

I blinked at the sun, hot overhead, and beating down on me with unrelenting power.

My face felt like it was in an oven. I calculated I had about three or four hours before I collapsed.

I was sure death would follow soon after.

SEVEN

I spent some time cursing the people who left me in the desert. That helped clear out some of my anger, but not all of it.

The sun was high over some nearby mountains. The ground was dry and granular. Some cactus poked up out of the ground here and there, but not enough to call where I was a forest, by any means. Instead, I was in a mostly barren environment.

The tracks of the truck that had left went off to the distant horizon.

How did they think this was a humane thing to do? I was without water or shelter. I didn't even have a shirt, let alone a hat.

My throat already felt parched. I looked around.

In the distance, I saw a fence. A long fence. And tall. It was solidly built, I could see that, and it offered good shade. I went toward it.

Walking was still difficult. My broken leg, I assumed, was mending itself, but it was taking a long time. Much longer than I wanted it to. Not anyone's fault, just the way of the world, I suppose. Just how things ended up. A long chain of events from the first synthesized amino acids back billions of years ago, then all the mutations and amendments, the punctuated jumps in complexity, carrying all the errors and misjudgments of nature with it, until it got to me. Whatever I was. Some kind of chimera? A mistake? A happy accident?

It was hard to tell. Surely there was a reason for my hybrid look.

Once I got to the fence, it proved to be just as refreshing as I had hoped it would be. Not exactly *cool* by any means, but appreciably lower in temperature. It was a relief.

As I stood there, tall enough to peer over the fence, I poked my head across the top of it, being careful to not let the coiled barbed wire at the summit touch my face, I saw a city. Or, at least, a town.

My tail snapped up. My legs trembled. I shuffled back and forth along the fence, frustrated that I could not jump over it.

Or could I?

I had not tested myself in this way. I had power, I knew that. Maybe I could use it to clear this fence?

No. Impossible. Not with my broken leg. I needed intact limbs to attempt anything like that.

I stepped back from the fence and looked in both directions. It seemed to go on to the horizon and beyond. This fence was long.

And it was solid. Metal posts sunk into the ground.

40   A man with two guns

The cross beams also of metal, bolted and welded into place. I would need tools to dismantle it.

I despaired of actually surviving this portion of my life. But since I'm writing this, you know I did survive, so I'll spare you the false suspense.

As I was standing there, considering the possibility of walking to the end of the fence but mostly resigned to my imminent demise, I heard the sound of a vehicle coming from the other side.

I poked my head over the fence and saw a tail feather of dust way down the road approaching me.

I waved.

The dust came closer and presently I discerned a vehicle in front of the dust. It was a jeep. Colored a dark green.

I did not know who was driving, what they were doing here, or what their intentions were, obviously, but I had no choice, really. If I did not get some assistance, I was going to perish.

So I raised my hands high and waved in the direction of the vehicle and the dust.

Both slowed as they got close to me, then the vehicle stopped. It was just on the other side of the fence.

The man driving the jeep wore a hat and looked like he was armed for war. He had two guns strapped to his sides and I saw more firearms in the seat next to him. I don't know what he was prepared for, but if I needed protection from whatever it was, it appeared this was the right guy.

The door opened. A man stepped out. He held a gun, and he pointed it at me.

"You're a tall one," he said. "What you doing there?"

"I'm in trouble," I said. "I need water. And food. And clothes. I'm going to burn up out here."

The man couldn't see through the fence, which meant he didn't know I was part horse.

He spit on the ground. "You've got some troubles," he said, "that's for sure. But it's got nothing to do with me."

"Granted," I said. I saw that he was without anything resembling a generous nature. He was more inclined to help himself, I suppose, than attempt to add to the empathy of the world. "But I can make it worth your while."

"You got a fat wallet hidden somewhere on you?"

"No," I said.

"Then what you got I could possibly want?"

"Have you ever wanted to see a mythical creature?"

He didn't answer. Just gripped the pistol a little harder. "You shittin' me?"

I shook my head. "Absolutely not. Few people get to see a centaur."

"A what?"

"A centaur. Half man. Half horse."

Now he stepped back. I suppose being close to a crazy person can make anyone a little skittish.

"I think I'll just get back in my vehicle and leave you to the buzzards," he said.

Lure of easy money

He gripped the door handle of his jeep and was about to pull it open.

"Look," I said, "it's simple. Just take a peek over the fence. You'll see."

He waved his hand, dismissing me.

"You could make a million dollars with me. Easy. Maybe more."

This stopped him. He let go of the handle and rubbed his forefinger against his thumb. That seemed to generate the requisite interest and change in his brain.

"That right?"

"I am not shitting you," I said. "Park your vehicle next to the fence, then climb up and look over the fence. You'll see."

I truly did not believe he was going to do any such thing, but he surprised me. He did move the jeep next to the fence. Then he pointed the gun at me and asked me to move down a few paces. I did so. Far enough that there was about twenty feet of fence between me and his vehicle on the other side. I then watched as he got up on the roof and looked over the fence, being careful, as I had been earlier, to keep the barbed wire from cutting him.

He looked across at me.

I pranced a little, making my legs do a kind of shuffle and dance.

He whistled. Long and hard.

"Told you," I said.

"You for real?"

"As real as you."

He stared some more. I turned around, shook my tail at him, and kept turning until I was facing him again.

"You wait right there," he said.

"That was the plan all along," I said.

I heard his jeep crunch on the desert gravel, then a short time later a rope with a metal hook on the end came over the fence so it landed on my side.

I trotted over to the hook. "What you want me to do with this?" I asked.

"Wrap it around the top of one of the posts," he said.

"Really?" I asked.

"Yes, really," he said.

I bent down, witch was no easy task. My body didn't like to bend there where my horse part met my human part, but with some difficulty I picked up the hook and then it was a delicate process to loop the cable with the hook over the end of the post. I had to be careful not to cut myself on barbed wire.

I didn't succeed. I got three or four cuts, which only made me curse, loudly.

The man on the other side snickered. "Mythological creatures have dirty mouths," he said. "Who knew?"

I shrugged. "I get frustrated, just like anyone. You have a first aid kit in that jeep?"

"Of course. I'm always prepared."

"I could use some bandages." Blood was running down my arms.

 The fence yields

"All in good time. Let's get you onto this side first."

"Fine," I said.

I secured the hook around the cable, then stepped back.

"Perfect," he said. He got into his jeep, put it into gear, and slowly inched his vehicle forward. The cable tightened to a taut line. The jeep worked its power over the ground, sending up dust and making gouges in the ground. The wheels started spinning.

I didn't think the man's plan was going to work, and was just about to tell him, when the jeep suddenly gained sufficient traction to begin pulling the post over.

It moved slowly at first, groaning against the force of the cable. I heard metal splinter and snap. The fence cross beams began to bend.

It was something of a miracle to watch the fence gradually but steadily begin to lean.

"Wow," I said.

The man stopped the engine and smiled at me. "All in a day's work," he said.

"You wreck fences all the time?"

"Only when necessary," he said. "To get people across the border."

"What's this a border of?"

"You dim witted or something?"

"Just new."

As we talked, he unhooked the cable and had me wrap it around the next post over.

"It's the border between New Mexico and Texas."

I knew they were states in the union. Or thought I did.

"Why would there be a fence? Aren't they in the same country?"

"Not for a while. Not since Texas broke away. They're their own country now."

I took this in as I secured the loop. "What side am I on?"

"New Mexico."

"You're trying to get me into Texas?"

"Isn't that what you wanted?"

It wasn't. Not exactly. But I felt I had no choice.

"Now you just sit still," he said. "I'll have you on the right side in half a second."

He worked his jeep and made the post lean over, just like he did with the other one.

The cross beams leveled out and I saw a path to—I suppose—something resembling freedom. Or at least sanctuary.

But something smelled bad about the whole enterprise and I suddenly didn't want to do what he was asking me to do.

He got out of his jeep and stood in front of it. "Well," he said. "Come on. You have a clear path."

I started walking. Took two steps, then stopped. "What's the problem?" he asked. "Come on. You can just step over the barbed wire."

I licked my lips. If I stayed on my side, I was surely go-

 I am a target yet again

ing to perish. But if I went with him, well, I didn't want to think of what my fate might be.

"I've changed my mind," I said.

His hand went to his side and he pulled out one of his guns and pointed it at me. "I've put in a lot work, here," he said. "I've risked jail time by damaging this fence. You're coming with me."

His hand was rock steady and he looked right at me. He had a clear shot and I was pretty sure that if I didn't comply, I was going to have to endure something worse than a few cuts on my arm and hands. I was going to have deal with at least one bullet in me, maybe more.

I took two steps back. Then another one. He extended his arm even further and took aim.

"Don't push me," he said. "I'm not afraid to use this."

"If you kill me, I can't get you your million dollars."

"Your body will get me as much. Maybe more."

I hadn't considered that. But I wasn't about to surrender to him. If he wanted to shoot me, then that was the way it was.

I took two more steps back.

"You leave me no choice," he said.

Then he pulled the trigger.

EIGHT

I guess the best you could say about him was that he had all the right intentions for his own cause. He was ready to kill for what he wanted. I was beginning to realize that such a stance was considered respectful and proper in the land I had found myself in.

But his aim was weaker than his intentions. The bullet whistled past my ear and must have ended up a long way away, eventually falling to the ground and maybe startling a jack rabbit or a coyote.

It also made me jump. I lost all composure and turned and ran from the man and the fence. My body was ready to fly, but instead I kind of hobbled, given my injury.

I was fully prepared to feel bullets in my back, but that didn't happen. Instead I heard a few cracks of another firearm. Then a muffled yelp from the man, and silence.

I twisted around to look over my back end and I saw two guys on horseback coming in my direction. It took my mind a moment to untangle the situation. One of them had a net. He rode up close to me, which wasn't difficult, considering my condition, and tossed a net in my direction.

I tried to duck out of its way, but that didn't work. Instead, the net fell on me and tangled itself around my arms and neck, and then fell over my hide and down to my feet, where it tangled me up pretty good. Good enough that I stopped running.

The guy who threw the net, then cinched it tight around me. The other guy came riding up and put a noose around my neck.

"What a second," I said. "That isn't necessary."

48   I assess my situation

They weren't inclined to pay me any heed. They were about to cinch the noose tight, when I reached up and managed to push it over my head. That just seemed to make the guy mad. He picked up the rope from the ground and tossed it up and over my head so that it fell down my side and then when the guy cinched it again, it trapped my arms at my sides so I couldn't move them.

"Easy, there," said one of the guys. Then the other guy repeated the same words.

"Easy, nothing," I said. "Let go of me."

"I don't think so, man," said the first one.

"Did you shoot the other guy?"

"Sure we did," said the second one. "He was going to shoot you. Tried to shoot you, actually."

I was breathing hard and the air was so dry and hot that it was hurting my lungs. Running, even at the crawling speed I was running at, took a lot of energy and the blood all had to be routed through my little lungs before they could go to my equine portions. I was a being of one horse-power, but I was not a being with the proper biological apparatus to service that one horsepower in any meaningful way. I was never going to be able to run like a real horse. The energy requirements were just too high.

"And what do you want with me?"

They laughed. Both of them. "Want with you? What makes you think we want anything from you?"

"You captured me for a reason." I tried to strain against

my ropes, but they were too strong. Also, I was weak from running.

"You talk a lot," said the first guy. "I think maybe now it's a good time you should shut up. Understand?"

I understood. The guy with the rope yanked on it so I was twisted around and my feet shuffled in the sand.

He was not the least bit delicate about taking me where he wanted. We returned to the fallen fence, and there he tied me to one of the upright posts.

I looked beyond the post and saw the first guy, the one who had shot at me. He was on the ground. Blood pooled around him and soaked into the ground, turning it dark and ugly. I was sure he was dead, but I didn't dare ask my new captors.

They both laughed. "In case you're wondering," said one of them, "he really is dead."

I kept silent.

"Isn't the first one we've killed, either. So don't think you're safe. Don't think we're going to have second thoughts about putting a slug into you. If we have to."

I had no such thought, but my hearts were beating so fast I thought they might jump out of both my chests.

Then the other guy put a saddle on me. It was made of heavy leather and it felt like a huge weight on me.

"Hey," I said.

"Hey, nothing," said one of the guys. "Hold still."

He buckled the saddle against my horse belly and

cinched it good and tight. Tight enough that I felt like I was going to break a rib. Maybe I did, for all I knew.

"You ever do any racing?" one of the them asked.

"Racing?"

"Horse racing."

"I'm not a horse."

"Yeah, right. Answer the question. You ever in any kind of horse race anywhere?"

"I'm not good for that. I've got a bum leg. And I have to breathe through a human nose and mouth. I could never get enough oxygen to sustain any kind of running."

He slapped me across the mouth. I reeled. He laughed. "Now listen to me," he said. "I didn't ask you if you were a winner. Just if you raced. That's all."

I shook my head.

He grunted. "Well," he said, "we're going to have to teach you how."

He turned from me, which was his mistake.

As he presented his side to my reach, I was suddenly able to wrestle my arms free, and I grabbed one of the guns from his holster and held it up and pointed it at him.

"Well, well, well," he said. "Got some spirit in you."

I pulled the trigger. I did not hesitate. I was ready to kill. It felt right.

But nothing happened. No recoil. No shot. No bullet. Nothing.

I felt a blow on the back of my head.

Must have been the other guy.

Then I saw nothing.

NINE

I was starting to get tired of waking up in strange places.

Strong smells invaded my nostrils as I opened my eyes to semidarkness. I was standing up, which was good, but I was also in a stall. A horse stall.

I heard other horses in adjoining stalls. They raspberried their lips and twitched their hides.

My own horse parts were similarly unruly. My skin undulated and rolled and shook.

I trotted over to the stall door and saw that it was locked with a padlock. No way out.

Or was there?

I looked around for a tool. Or even a key. Sawdust covered the dirt floor. The gate was made of metal. On the other side of the gate I saw a shovel leaning against the wall. I reached over the gate but could not get within more than a foot of it.

If I did not have a horse half, it would have been no problem at all to simply leap over the gate. There was enough room for a man. But not for a man/horse hybrid.

I kicked the gate for all I was worth. Didn't do much, except make my hoof hurt.

I leaned over the top of the gate and tried to reach for the shovel. My arms extended as far as I could go. I bent at the line where my horse part joined my human part.

As I did so, I noticed that my body was thin. Much thinner than I had remembered it.

The horse part had skin that was loose and wrinkled in place. My human part was thin as well, with bones prominent.

But I couldn't get to the shovel. It was just out of my grasp.

I strained harder than I should have, and I think I bruised my belly.

I stopped trying and backed away from the gate. I rubbed my belly and tried to think what to do next. There was a bin with hay in it at one side of the stall. I still felt like I wanted hay. I still had the craving that I remembered when I first came to consciousness on the trail. But that craving did not make my mouth water. It gave me sensations in my horse section. It was like I wanted the hay there, but I didn't want the hay to travel through the necessary channels to get there.

And yet.

Hunger is a powerful motivator.

I picked up some of the hay. It was dry and fibrous. I rolled stalks of it between my thumb and fingers. I tried to crumble it, but it wouldn't. It remained as stalks.

I put some on my tongue. No taste. Or, rather, a kind of bland taste, like eating paper.

I tried chewing. It was tough going. The fibrous nature of the stuff made it necessary to chew and chew and chew.

I demand nourishment  53

My mouth twisted into a grimace. The taste was so bland as to be repulsive.

I spit it out.

I could not sustain myself on this. My horse insides screamed in revolt. They wanted that hay. Needed it.

I called out to the door on the other side of the stall. "Hey!" I said. "Get me some food. Some real food. Is anyone there?"

No one answered. There were other stalls, with horses. No centaurs. They were arrayed next to me in a long line. What were we doing there?

I retreated to the wall on the other side of the gate. It appeared to be relatively thin. Could I?

I wasn't sure. But I had to try. I put my hand on the wall and braced myself against it with strength. I pushed. Hard.

The wall did bend a little, but not very much.

Next, I put my horse end right next to the wall.

I noticed, just in passing, that my rear leg had been healed. Not sure how that happened, but the bandage and cast was gone. The leg moved very well. It was as though it had never been broken.

I began throwing my weight against the wall in a rocking motion, hitting it again and again and again. I made noise. I rocked the stall for all I was worth.

Nothing much was happening. I wasn't putting a hole in the wall, or making it buckle.

But I kept going. I figured I had nothing to lose. I did

this for a long time. Probably a good five minutes, not letting up on the wall at all.

When I stopped I was breathing hard. Sweat was pouring off me and I felt more fatigued than I had been since I arrived.

I was also thirsty. I saw bottles of water next to the hay. I opened one and drank it down in several gulps. I felt the coolness of it go down my throat to my stomach, my human stomach, then I felt trickles of it continue past that to my horse stomach.

I wondered at the peculiarity of having two stomachs. That wasn't right, somehow. It meant that I was not really one creature, but a hybrid. Nature would not have designed me this way. I must have been made. By who, I couldn't say. Some demented scientist working in some crazy government project.

Maybe.

As I was contemplating the possibilities, I heard a sound on the roof.

Footsteps. Human footsteps.

Then particles from the ceiling came down on me. A moment later, the ceiling was crumbling. Big pieces fell around me. I put my hands over my head and ducked down to avoid whatever was causing the ruckus and then a figure dropped through the ceiling and stood before me.

"I'm here to rescue you," she said. Then she pulled out a set of snips from her backpack and cut the padlock on my stall door. The door swung open.

She slapped my side. "Giddy-up," she said.

I took two steps closer, but didn't go through.

"I'm scared," I said. "I don't think I'm ready for freedom."

TEN

She laughed and laughed. Doubled over with laughter. I didn't see the joke, so I waited for her to finish.

Then she looked through the stall door at two people holding cameras on their shoulders, which had been pointed at me. I had not noticed them up to that moment.

"What is this?" I asked.

She shrugged. "Just a bit of play acting," she said.

Other people came into the barn. They were carrying plates laden with food. Spaghetti, roast chicken, sweet potatoes, heaps of vegetables, rice, and I don't know what else.

They brought it to me and I grabbed some of it up with my hands, not waiting for utensils, and stuffed food into my mouth and chewed happily and swallowed and then stuffed more.

"Whoa, there," she said. "Slow down. You'll hurt yourself."

"I can't slow down," I said. "I have a horse half to feed."

She let me continue. I had no shame attached to my ravenous appetite or the way I was catering to it. I needed to eat food. Lots of it.

56   I am distracted by food

"You know what's going on?" she asked.

I found a plate of hamburgers. Three of them. I ate one in three bites and then grabbed up some soda and downed that to wash the food through my system.

I shook my head.

"I'm Loretta Fields. Lori. I have a TV show. It's called *ESCAPE!*. We help people get out of unlawful incarceration."

"Is that so?" I said as I chewed my way through a second hamburger.

"Normally we get prisoners out of jail. We try to concentrate on the ones that were wrongfully convicted."

"This is a TV show?" I asked.

"Underground," she said. "We're not exactly mainstream. Not yet. We have a lot of viewers though. One of these days we're going to be legit. Until then." She shrugged and smiled at me. "We do what we can."

Since she had brought me ample supplies of food, I was inclined to not only listen to her, but think of her as my savior.

"Here," she said. "Take a look."

I glanced up from my eating and saw a monitor that she had pulled in front of me. I saw the screen light up from darkness with a splashy logo made from the letters of the word ESCAPE that pushed against the boundaries of a box surrounding them. Then, as the letters burst through the box and careened to the edge of the screen, the logo and lettering faded to an image of—

—me.

I was being hustled away from the facility where I was gelded and put onto a truck. A voice over prattled on about the power of myth to escape any incarceration.

I stopped chewing the fries that someone had put next to another plate of burgers.

"This has all been a TV show?"

Lori nodded. "What do you think?"

"I think you people are sick. I want to call the police."

Here she laughed. "The police don't care about you! You're not even human."

"I think I'm going to leave now," I said.

"You're free to go, for sure," she said. "We've opened the pen for you."

I stepped toward the stall door.

"Only thing is," she said, "where are you going to go? Where are you going to find people to feed you? Constantly, as you say."

"I'll manage."

"Like you managed to get your manhood—if that's what we should call it—dispensed with?"

"You trying to get me riled up or something?"

The person holding the camera had it right in my face. Close up. Obviously interested in getting my reactions on film.

"And where do you get off putting my image on screen? How can you just co-opt my life for your stupid TV show?"

She looked at me, while my face turned red, I was sure.

 # Seduced by pizza

While I emoted and kicked and gestured with my arms. I was animated and angry. Nothing that had happened to me thus far had gotten me so riled up.

She smiled. "Did you get that Ray?"

The camera operator smiled. "Sure did," he said.

"Excellent," she said, then put a hand out to my shoulder to pat it.

"This is unbelievable," I said. "All you're interested in is getting me emotional for your show."

"Got me there," she said. "But we feed you!"

I smelled pizza, and turned around. Someone was holding two large pies in boxes. The fragrance made my knees wobble. All four of them.

I grabbed one of the boxes, lifted it open and took out a slice, laden with vegetables, bacon, pineapple, and pepperoni, and downed it in three bites. Just like with the hamburger. Then I took another slice.

"I should get an agent," I said. "Or a manager. I'm obviously important to your show. I should have representation."

"Listen," she said, "I appreciate what you're saying, but think about it. Mythical creatures don't have managers."

"Maybe they should."

She tapped her foot, and narrowed her eyebrows. "Here's what you need to understand," she said. "You're at grave risk."

The pizza was almost gone by then. I knew I was hungry, but I had no idea how much food I could actually put away. It was epic in itself. Ray kept filming, not missing a moment.

"What risk?"

"Are you kidding me? You're a monster. Some kind of hybrid. No one knows where you came from, but there are theories. You were concocted in some mad scientist's lab. Cloned from a man and a horse, then thrown together. Or the manifestation of some collective unconscious symbol. Jungification, if you will."

"Yeah, so?"

"So there are a lot people who don't care for that kind of thing. You are a target, my friend. Lots of people want to shoot you."

I had already experienced that. More than once. "But some of that was staged," I said.

She tapped her foot and looked away.

"Right? I'm right, aren't I?"

"Partially," she said.

"I knew it. That guy at the fence. He wasn't actually dead. It was an act. Right? *Right*?"

I wanted it to be true. I wanted them to know I wasn't some rube who could be duped. I could see through their ridiculous act.

She glanced over at Ray, then tapped some buttons on the keyboard next to the screen. I saw another episode of *ESCAPE!* cue up. This one was shot from high over head. A desert scene. Dots of green that I took to be cactus. A dark line across the middle. Must have been shot with a

60   I spike the ratings

drone. Then the image zoomed in. The dark line resolved itself to become the fence I had been deposited next to. And there I was, being chased by the two guys.

The man that had struck the deal with me was on the ground, blood pooled behind him. They followed me, the drone tracking my flight away from the fence, but then it cut back, momentarily to the man on the ground.

It zoomed in on his face, which was turned to the side. Even though it was not a front shot, I recognized that face.

I looked at Ray. He smiled back at me.

"You!" I said.

"The very same. We're a tight operation. Everyone pitches in."

I looked at Lori, who was beaming. "We were proud of that episode," she said. "Very realistic. Our ratings spiked."

As I was watching these televised episodes of my life, I began to feel a burning inside me. It was a combination of anger and a profound feeling of futility. I was nothing to them but a road to ratings. They would feed me till I burst, just as long as they could record the bursting.

"I'm no criminal," I said.

"We know that. We're moving our show's focus. No more convicted killers sprung from jail. Now it's all you. We'll protect you from the crazies, just as long as you agree to let us stage more of these."

"Escapes," I said. "You want a new escape every week."

"That's it exactly."

She and Ray both beamed at me, like we were all three in collusion against a common enemy.

"I don't think so," I said.

I turned from them and pushed the stall gate open and stepped into the open barn.

"You're going to regret it," said Lori.

I didn't look back.

Instead, I walked to the barn door. On the other side I saw a clear blue sky, fleeced with a few clouds here and there, and green hills. I walked toward that vision.

I heard Ray and Lori arguing with each other. Something about what a mistake it was to reveal to me what they had done.

I dropped a few large turds as I walked. Symbolically telling them what I thought of them and their show.

Then I stepped through the door.

I felt cool air rush over me. The sensation was welcome and refreshing. It was as though I was coming home.

I lifted my arms high.

That's when I heard the shots. Several of them. I was so startled, I didn't know where to run. Wood splintered behind me as rounds hit the barn.

I quickly scanned the horizon, looking for where the shots had come from.

Nothing.

Then I heard a buzzing sound and I looked up. Several drones were circling around me.

Then they opened fire with a vengeance.

ELEVEN

The dirt around me erupted in a forest of dust bursts. The shots filled my ears. I bolted and ran. It was probably not the best thing to be doing. I should have gone back into the barn, but I had no wish to return to the arms of Lori and Ray. If I was going to die, then let it be by these drones, not the insane people who wanted to help me while incarcerating me.

As I ran away from the barn, I saw that the drones were not following me. Instead, they advanced on the barn and began shooting at it. There were also some vehicles outside the barn which received a rich treatment of munitions. They were covered with holes.

Once I was sure I was no longer the target—if I ever was—I stopped. My lungs hurt and I was panting for air. I put my hands on my forelegs and bent over and gulped air.

As I did so, a peculiar sensation invaded my being. I felt like I had my hands on human thighs. It was an eerie feeling. I had not felt it before, but by merely touching my equine forelegs, I conjured up in my mind two phantom limbs: my human legs.

I did not rise from that position, instead choosing to savor this feeling. It was as though I had found a completely new room in a house, one that had been hidden from the inhabitants of that house for years. Maybe decades.

I contain ghosts 63

When I stood up again, my phantom human limbs were still there. They seemed to exist just a few inches in front of my equine limbs. They didn't reach the ground. After all, they were shorter than horse forelegs, but they were there. When I shifted my awareness only slightly, I felt like they were my true legs and I was floating on air.

I pause the narrative here to go into some detail on the sensations because it feels important to understand that this was the point at which I first felt like a mythical being. Before discovering my phantom limbs, I felt like a mistake. A blunder, either of nature's doing, or of some demented animal engineer.

But now, I saw I harbored ghosts. I was possibly haunted. Or maybe I was actually two consciousnesses in one. I did not know which, but I knew it felt exhilarating, like I truly was something strange and exalted.

That feeling of euphoria lasted for more than a few minutes. I stood and watched the barn being torn up. Eventually the drones must have exhausted their supply of ammunition, because the shooting stopped.

My ears rang with the aftershocks of those shots. The air was ragged with the fading echoes. I felt like I was in the grips of some strange power that the drones had unleashed. They continued to circle, in their buzzing way, above the barn for several seconds. Then they each, in turn, stopped circling and headed in a straight line away from the barn.

I watched them recede in single file, like overly regi-

 # Ray under suspicion

mented birds, and then I turned my attention back to the barn.

It remained still and silent.

Soon, though, the front door slid open and Ray emerged and stood near the door and looked up. He shielded his eyes from the glare of the sky, then lowered them and scanned the horizon. He pointed at me.

"Wait," he said.

My instinct was to run, but I quelled it.

He began walking toward me.

He had not been hurt, as far as I could tell, but he looked shaken up. And why not? He had just been subject to a particularly nasty attack from flying killing machines. Anyone would be at least a little shaken up by such an experience.

It took him a couple of minutes to reach me.

I greeted him with a nod of my head. "Ray," I said.

"You order that hit?" he asked.

"What?"

"Was that you? Did you figure a way to attack us?"

I shook my head. "You've got me all wrong if you think I did that. I almost got hit myself."

He looked at me suspiciously.

I put up my hands. "Swear to God."

"You believe in God?"

"It's just an expression."

He stared at me, like he wanted to see through me. I stared right back.

"We were trying to help you," he said.

"You were helping yourselves," I said. "And your show. I was just a means to that."

"Tomato tomahto."

I laughed. "Look. How could I have organized anything like what just happened? I've been incarcerated or out of it since I got here. Wherever here is."

He looked up at the sky. Scanning it for possible new attacks?

"Anyone hurt inside?" I asked.

He shook his head. "We were all just scared. The rest of the crew doesn't want to come outside."

"I don't blame them."

"Rival networks have tried to sabotage us before, but there was never anything like this. This is war, man. They were trying to kill us."

"But they didn't," I said. "Probably just a warning."

He regarded me with skepticism.

"You really are naïve, aren't you?"

"Yup," I said.

"Lori wants to quit the show. Never thought she'd be afraid of the competition."

"What about you? You want to quit the show?"

"The show saved my life. I was in jail for something I didn't do. She got me out."

"So you were an episode of *ESCAPE!*?

He nodded.

"So you're probably wanted by the police."

He nodded again. "The show is my shelter. Lori hired me soon after she sprung me."

Ray looked like a bewildered little boy, unsure of what to do next, or even how to figure out what to do next.

"Listen," I said, "I think I know what you're going through. You're lost in a world you no longer understand."

"What?" he asked.

"Think about it. If *ESCAPE!* goes, you don't have a family anymore. You'll be adrift. That's exactly what's happened to me. No one knows what to do with me. I've been shot at more times than I care to tell you. Far as I can tell, the world doesn't want or need me. Yet here I am. Now I have to decide what to do about it."

The buzzing was coming back. I heard it over the horizon. Ray heard it too.

"What is that?" he asked.

"They're returning," I said. "Probably went for reinforcements. Or to reload."

Ray looked terrified. I didn't blame him. "They're going to kill us for sure, this time."

From the barn, the rest of the crew came streaming out. They ran toward us.

Ray wanted to go back to them. I could see it in his face. The shelter of something familiar, even if it was dangerous, was pulling him.

The drones were almost upon us.

"They're after them," I said. "Not you."

"As far as you know," he said, "which isn't much."

"You got one chance," I said. "Get on my back and I'll take you away from all this."

He wavered. I didn't get it. The drones were after the crew of *ESCAPE!*

The drones opened fire. They sent puffs of dust in lines that went toward the crew. The crew scattered.

One of the drones peeled away from the rest of the group. It headed toward us.

Ray, seeing this at the same time I did, grabbed my hand. I helped him up. He straddled my back and I kicked into speed away from the drone.

TWELVE

The drone, apparently, was not intent on us. It did, however, tear up the sky above us as it sped above our heads.

Ray kept his head down as I galloped. The sound of my hoofs on the desert sand was strangely soothing, like a lullaby was playing in our heads.

"You okay back there?" I asked.

He grunted. At a loss for words, I suppose. He had his hands around my chest. I didn't like that, but what else was he going to do?

The drone kept going, then took a sharp dive and crashed into the ground. I saw dust come up, but no flames.

"Let's go see what was on that thing," I said.

"Shouldn't we go somewhere else?" asked Ray.

"You have some place in mind?"

"I got a place in Santa Fe."

"We can go there after," I said.

He seemed doubtful. "I don't know," he said.

But he didn't have any say in the matter. I was the one in charge. I increased my speed. Not by much, but enough that we both noticed.

I felt Ray's fear. It came up from him like the stench from a garbage pit.

I, on the other hand, had no fear. I was flying. My legs worked under me like parts of a machine. I barely touched the ground, but it was enough to keep me in flight. The air whistled past my ears and over my arms and chest, and continued to my horse's body.

As we approached the downed drone, I slowed my pace.

"Be careful," said Ray.

"You want out," I said, "now's the time. I don't need you."

"And I don't need you," he said.

I didn't answer. No point.

The drone was definitely broken. It was about three feet wide, and the edge of it was torn. Shredded. The middle, which was a bulgy approximation of a sphere, was mostly intact, but it no longer looked lethal. Funny how being broken on the ground can change all that.

Its gun barrels were also bent, and I saw that there was

a long skid mark, which mean it slid along the ground before it came to a stop.

Ray slipped off me and we both approached the drone.

"You think there's anything here we can use?" he asked.

"Get the guts of the thing," I said. "The computer parts in the middle."

He got a stick and poked at the thing. I heard some glass pieces scrape against each other.

"What was that?" I asked.

"Probably the eye in the sky," he said.

"You broke it on purpose?"

He nodded. "No need letting it spy on us anymore."

"I don't think it was doing anymore spying."

"Never know," he said.

"You know any software experts?" I asked. "Anyone that can find out what was in this thing's flight path? What it was supposed to be doing?"

Ray got on his knees and tried to peel back part of the drone to get to the center of it. He couldn't manage it.

"Hey," he said, "put your hoof here."

I trotted forward and placed my front leg on the spot he indicated. "Like that?" I asked. I was pressing down on one edge of the drone.

"Yeah," he said, then put his fingers into a small gap and gripped the edge. "Now push," he said.

I pushed. I pinned the drone to the ground. He pulled and grunted and peeled back the covering to reveal some circuity underneath.

"Bingo," he said.

"Can you pull out any of those components?"

He reached in and grabbed some of them. He put them in his pocket.

"Anything else you want to grab?"

He walked around the drone and flipped it over. The wings were bent and the rotors that kept it aloft like a helicopter looked like lengths of silver ribbon that had been through a shredder.

"No," he said.

"Then let's get out of here," I said.

He stood next to me while we both looked down at the broken craft. I felt an absurd wish to say something about its passing. Maybe offer some consoling words to its relatives.

Don't know where that came from.

And while I was looking at it, a peculiar sensation creeped over me. I suddenly felt like my torso and head were wrong for my body. And my arms! They were ridiculous. Like a beard on a pig. They needed to go.

I tossed my head and whinnied. Wind ruffled my mane. What?

All this was startling enough, but then I let air out that rattled my lips. What was that?

My ears rotated.

I had another phantom in me. This was a horse's head. Whatever had made me had not figured out a way to keep the phantoms out of me. I had phantom human parts and also phantom horse parts.

Ray turned from the drone and faced me. His features went dark. I saw fear in his eyes.

"What is it?" I asked.

He pointed past me. I turned around. Three people carrying fearsome-looking weapons advanced toward us.

They didn't look like they were friendly. Not in the least.

THIRTEEN

I must say, I was getting a little tired of all the guns that seemed to be trained on me all the time. Didn't people have better things to do with their time?

Ray put his hands in the air.

I did the same.

Seemed like the right thing to do. Like this was some kind of ritual.

The figures were dressed in saffron colored robes, and their faces were covered.

"What ho?" I asked. "I'd appreciate it if you didn't point those things at us."

That didn't change anything. The weapons were still trained on us. Two on me, if my observation skills were at all reliable, and one on Ray. He cowered. I didn't like that. Didn't like that my ally was so afraid. I needed better than that.

They indicated with the end of their barrels that Ray should move closer to me.

He did so. I heard a whimper from him.

"Get it together," I said in a low voice.

"Shut up," said one of the three.

I spread my hands and said nothing, though I did tilt my head to the side and widen my eyes. It felt right. Like a universal sign of falling into line. I figured I didn't need to rile them up any.

Inside, though, I was plenty steamed. Just when things looked like they might tilt in my direction for once, these bozos show up.

"Give us the parts of the drone," they said.

Ray moved to do as they asked. I stopped him. "We don't have any of them," I said.

"Don't fuck with us," said the central figure. "We know you broke it open. Now give us the goods."

"You want stuff from that drone," I said, "you get them yourself."

Their heads tilted down slightly, as though they were examining the drone.

Ray was shaking beside me. "It's okay," I whispered to him. "Just be cool."

"I'm not used to being under attack," he whispered back to me.

"I am," I said. "It's been the most predictable part of my life here so far."

"I can't take this anymore," he said.

"Don't do anything," I said.

The three looked back up at us. "What's all that talking?" they asked.

"Nothing," I said.

Ray stepped forward. "I don't know this guy," he said.

The anger inside me only grew when he said that sentence. My phantom anti-centaur, the thing inside me that was a man's body with a horse's neck and head, erupted out of me and fell upon Ray.

I was the only one of the five of us that saw him. The others, all four of them, were dumbfounded as my phantom fell upon Ray and knocked him over to the ground.

"What's going on?" asked one of the saffron covered guys.

My phantom didn't stop with Ray. It proceeded to knock over the central one of the saffron robed. He sprawled on the ground, completely mystified as to what just happened to him.

The anti-centaur was a ghostly blur in the air. He stepped on the man on the ground, who released his weapon and lifted his hands up to his head to try to protect himself.

The other two guys pointed their weapons at me, then at Ray, still out of commission on the ground, then back to me again.

"You're looking in the wrong place," I said, actually enjoying the moment as the anti-centaur made a fist and punched the guy on the left right in the chin. He fell over backward. His weapon slipped out of his hand.

The last of the saffron-robed saw the three on the ground, and turned and ran. He was fast, too. I thought to follow him, but decided I didn't need to.

Instead, as my anti-centaur stomped on the two saffron guys, Ray scrambled up and came back to my side.

"What the fuck?" he said.

"Never mind that," I said. "Get the weapons."

Ray ran over to the discarded weapons and grabbed them up. He gave me one. I hefted it in my hands.

My anti-centaur was alternating kicking the guys, who were terrified more from the unseen nature of the attackers than from the actual beating they were getting.

Ray looked at them, writhing and crying out, and had no idea what to make of it, but after a short time he began to see the humor in the situation and laughed at them and pointed.

"They having seizures?" he asked.

"Good an explanation as any," I said.

The rifle felt strange in my hands. Maybe I really did need to have a bow and arrow. A bow was a weapon worthy of me. This firearm was more of a curiosity. I lifted it to my shoulder and sighted down the barrel and swung it toward a distant tree.

I fired.

The sound was piercing and sobering. Everyone in the vicinity, stopped, even my anti-centaur, which looked up at me with a questioning expression in his eyes, his horse eyes.

I blinked at him and he gave each of the downed men one more kick to the ribs, then came back to me, quickly, as though propelled by a strong wind.

I felt him slide back into the confines of my body, then he wiggled and locked himself into place.

Meanwhile, Ray lifted his weapon and aimed it at the two guys still on the ground.

"I don't know what just happened," he said, "but it looks like we have the upper hand now."

"Never mind that," I said. "Let's get going."

"But they were going to kill us."

"I seriously doubt that," I said.

"Cal," said Ray, "you don't know how things work here. They attacked us. They threatened us. We need to take care of them."

I was already preparing to walk away from the two downed guys, but Ray was talking nonsense, and I had to do something about that.

"Just get on my back," I said. "We'll get out of here and these guys will nurse their wounds and get themselves back on their feet and think about what happened here."

"Nothing doing," said Ray. "I got business to take care of."

"Ray," I said. "Think about this. I'm a famous person. People will know what I'm up to. If you're with me, they'll know what you're up to."

Friend becomes foe

"Yeah. So?"

He had his weapon trained on the head of the larger of the downed guys.

"So, you won't get away with murder."

"It's self defense."

"Not if you've got their weapons."

"That's right," said Ray. "*Their* weapons. Which they were going to use to shoot *us*."

"Ray," I said, "this is your last warning."

The guys on the ground had managed to move closer to each other and were huddled together in seating positions. They didn't have any visible wounds. After all, they were attacked by a phantom, but they sure looked as though they had wounds. They crouched in fearful positions. They cowered. And they looked like they were trying to sink into the ground.

Then Ray turned his weapon on me.

Inside I groaned. My phantom anti-centaur was ready to pounce.

"Looks like maybe my real enemy is you," said Ray. "Hope you have your will written."

He took a breath.

My anti-centaur would be too late.

I raised my weapon in self defense, but knew it was going to be too late as well.

Ray pulled the trigger.

FOURTEEN

A lot can happen between the time a trigger is pulled and a bullet finds its target.

You wouldn't think so, considering the sequence of events that a pulled trigger sets in motion. I certainly didn't think so before that time staring down the barrel controlled by Ray.

But there was time for my anti-centaur to leap out of me. It moved, in a flash, toward Ray and before Ray could see it or even hope to see it, it put itself between me and the bullet.

Things got very confusing after that.

I'm not here to tell you that the phantom stopped a bullet. That would be ridiculous. At the very least. I'm not even here to tell you that Ray had terrible aim. He was not that far from me. He had a clear shot. The weapon appeared to be functioning normally. The barrel was pointed directly at me.

And yet.

The bullet missed me. No pain, no ripping of flesh, no impact on my person. I dropped my hands and saw my phantom lying on the ground. Bleeding.

Ray looked down at his weapon, dumfounded, unwilling to believe he had missed.

He raised his weapon again, but this time I did not hesitate. I leaped toward him and grabbed the weapon from

78   I exercise some power

his hand and threw it aside. He cowered and fell over back-ward.

"You killed my twin," I said.

He looked up at me.

I reared back on my hind legs, clearly showing him I could trample him with my front legs. He raised his arms to protect himself and I came down, fast and hard, but made sure I did not land on him. My hoofs ended up on either side of his head.

He scrambled away from me and joined the two guys in saffron, still huddled together, still afraid.

The three of them looked like a pretty pathetic bunch.

My phantom twin had bled out. Only I could see it, I was sure. He had a hole in his head. Blood had soaked into the ground.

I went about and retrieved all the weapons and carried them under my arm. They were awkward, but I didn't want any of these three to be able to use them.

I extended my other hand toward Ray. "Give me the drone innards," I said.

I half expected resistance from him, but he had none. He reached into his pocket and handed me the circuit boards. I took them, then thought better of it.

"Give me your jacket," I said.

"No," he said.

I stepped toward him, making sure my hoofs were loud and kicked up a lot of dust. The threat was clear, I was pretty sure.

He took off his jacket and handed it to me. I didn't put it on, not just then, because holding the weapons was making that impossible. I stuffed the circuits into the pocket and hung the jacket over my other arm.

"We could have been a good team, Ray," I said. "But you had to get violent."

He shrugged. "Thanks for not killing me."

"I'm going to gallop away," I said. "After a few miles, I'll drop these weapons so you guys can follow me and get them back. I suppose you should have something to defend yourselves."

"Thanks," said Ray.

"Don't mention it."

I didn't give my phantom another thought. Mainly because I didn't know what it was for or where it came from or what, exactly, its purpose was. I felt no remorse. Certainly no grief. The thing saved my life, sure, but it was nothing. A ghost. A trifling. A wrinkle in the air. A bit of my psyche I didn't need anymore.

That's what I told myself, anyway. What I was really afraid of was feeling anything for the sad thing. I kind of wanted to bury it. But how do you bury a ghost? I didn't know. I didn't think anyone did.

I turned from the three men who had been intent on killing me and got going. I settled into a good fast-paced trot. I didn't know where I was going, and it didn't matter. I was a lost soul, wasn't I? Lost souls don't have homes. They are wanderers.

80   Destroying weapons

When I estimated I had gone about ten miles, I did as I had told the guys. I dropped the weapons on the ground.

Except, before that, I smashed each of them against rocks so they were broken and useless. That was a nice message to leave the three. If they even decided to follow my tracks. I was pretty sure they would. They seemed to really like their weapons. It seemed a lot of this world did.

By the time I had performed that little bit of subversion, the sun was low on the horizon, just getting ready to drop out of sight.

The air was cold, my stomach was empty. Actually, both of them were empty. I was more hungry than I could imagine, and I had no shelter and no prospects of any.

The land around me was flat and empty, except for some palo verde trees and a few saguaro. The wind, especially, seemed particularly fond of blowing over my skin and my fur.

I put on Ray's jacket. It afforded some protection, but not much. I really needed to get somewhere I could rest. And eat.

I kept walking. Darkness wrapped itself around me. I heard sounds in the night. Starlight lit my path, but not very well. I looked down and saw a murky gray mush, hardly anything to tell me that I was on solid ground, though my hoofs kept meeting solid ground with every step.

I heard panting around me. On all sides. I wasn't sure

what to make of this. Did the desert make sounds? Maybe I was making them and they were echoing back to me?

An owl flew over me. I saw its feathers in a faint glowing outline, as though someone had dripped paint on the edges, just enough to define them.

Along with the panting sounds, I suddenly heard faint beating sounds, like paws hitting the ground. There were dozens of them. They beat around me like a collection of drummers. Their sound rose up to my ears. I felt my fur rise up. My hide shivered.

I stopped. My breath was loud and ragged. I was scared, no doubt about it.

Then I saw animals. Many of them. They surrounded me. They had heads like dogs. Their legs were long and graceful, like a cat's legs, almost.

I counted quickly. Seven of them. And at least a few of them were growling at me.

Hungry coyotes. I was in the middle of a pack of hungry coyotes, and they were in no mood to negotiate my exit from their orbit of influence.

FIFTEEN

This account must feel like a series of dangerous encounters. It was not my intention to structure it so, but as I begin to see what has happened to me, I understand that no other form would capture the truth of my introduction to the world of 21st century America.

82   A howling good time

So indulge me while I recount the events that occurred after the coyotes made their intentions clear.

I had no phantom to aid me this time. Which was too bad, but which I could do nothing about.

All I had were my wits, and they had not served me particularly well to this point.

I cleared my throat and put back my head and howled into the night. I tried to make my howl sound like a coyote. I knew what they sounded like. I had heard them in my dreams. I worked my throat for all it was worth, singing a song that was designed to bring down the moon so I could hand it to the pack.

The growling stopped.

They joined in with the howling. We worked our respective vocal chords and sang a song for the ages.

As we sang, I began edging away from the center of the group. I knew this couldn't last, and their instinct for song was going to be superseded by their instinct for the hunt and the need to sate their hunger.

They seemed not to notice my movements, preoccupied as they were with their heads lifted to the heavens.

Despite my dire circumstances and my need to get away from them, I was more than unusually attuned to their wildness. It seemed as though I had found my tribe. Of a sort. I was singing to survive, it was true, but in the singing I also found a core spirit of untamed energy inside me.

I didn't know exactly where it resided. It felt like my

horse portion held it. After all, that was where the urge to run originated. Then, at the same time, it felt like my human chest—my heart—was also right there in the middle of the feeling.

The portion of me that was neither—or both—was where the two extremities met. There I felt a kind of ghostly mishmash. I wasn't sure what exactly my substance was there. I felt like I could break in two. Indeed, I would have been happy to do so. I could have fooled the pack by going in opposite directions.

My voice began to crack and waver. I wanted the energy to go on. I pulled up all the will I could and threw it into my voice and my throat. It was a supreme effort of will that I could not sustain. Not for long.

My song sputtered out.

By the time it did, I was actually outside the pack. I wanted to run, but I knew I could not outrun them all. Not without a much bigger head start.

The growling returned. The pack turned to me. I raised myself up on my hind legs and waved my front legs at them, hoping to instill some fear.

I briefly wondered where they were going to attack me first. Would it be my human part, at the throat? But that was high up. They couldn't jump that high. Or so I thought.

Maybe it would be my hindquarters. Attack me there and disable me. Make me fall to the ground and then go for my throat. I estimated I could last maybe a minute or two.

Were coyotes merciful? Did they go for the quick kill,

or did they toy with their prey, like cats. I felt curiously removed from the events about to overwhelm me. I had intellectual interest that somehow removed me from the center of consideration. It was as though my own mind knew I was a myth, and myths aren't personal. They're universal. They transcend the individual and move toward the larger view of creation, the one in which individuals don't really matter, except in the sense that an atom matters. Just part of the huge edifice.

As the pack's howling subsided and the growls returned with a vengeance, I had the fleeting thought that I was a fool for not keeping at least one of the weapons I had collected. I couldn't have shot all the coyotes, but one shot in the air and I bet they would have scattered to the wind.

I also missed my phantom double.

That had been a lucky accident.

As I stood with the pack ready to attack, I was not ready to die. I cried out for help. It felt futile, even as I said the word, drawn out and as loudly as I could, but my voice, it seemed, even in its diminished way, was all I had left.

The sound went across the landscape. The stars continued to look down on me.

The growling grew more fearsome. It snaked into me and entered my spine and crossed the seam where human joined with equine and went down my back all the way to my end, where it made my tail twitch with anticipation of something awful happening to me.

Circuit board sounds  85

I reached into the pocket of my jacket. There I fingered the pieces from the drone.

I pulled them out. Held them in my palm. They did have a certain *look* to them. It was almost as though—

I don't know what made me do it, but I brought one of the pieces up to my mouth. It was a layered circuit board; two green pieces of plastic sandwiching some metal wiring that curved and looped and seemed to be laying down some kind of hieroglyphic message.

I put it to mouth and blue as hard as I could.

The note that emerged was even more hair raising than the growls of the pack.

They must have felt something as well, because the growls immediately stopped.

I blew on the circuit boards again. The growling returned, but it was not an attack sound. It was more of a retreat signal. Or so I hoped.

The pack receded from me. I blew as hard as I possibly could, bringing up all the will I had left, all the air that was still in me, and sent it through the metal forest between the green plastic pieces.

The coyotes fled, running faster than I thought they had in them.

I was so relieved, I almost fell to the ground. My knees were so weak, I would have welcomed the fall.

But I was still cognizant of being in a dangerous area.

I turned and made my way in the opposite direction of the pack.

86 Weary of being attacked

I trudged through the night and the forest for some time. Easily an hour or so. I was in a wilderness area, or so it seemed to me. There were some faint glows on the horizon around me. I assumed those were from cities or towns, but I couldn't tell for sure, and they seemed a long way distant.

Then, as the sun was beginning to lighten the eastern sky even more than the city lights, I heard a sound I had hoped I would never hear again.

A gunshot. It hit my ears with an impact like a hammer.

I turned around.

A man on a horse was pointing a gun at me. I should have known, I suppose. I had had so many weapons trained on me by that time that it seemed the natural order of things in this part of the world.

"Hold it right there, mister," he said. "Or should I call you something else? You a man or an animal?"

"Neither," I said. "I'm just tired of all this."

Then I launched myself at full gallop in his direction, arms wide, wind billowing my hair, jacket rippling against my chest and arms, legs pounding the ground for all I was worth.

SIXTEEN

I knew I wasn't going to be happy about trampling the guy, but I didn't care. Not anymore. All I wanted was to have some kind of autonomy, some kind of life where I wasn't constantly being held at gunpoint.

I was perfectly willing, at that point, to die for that wish.

The guy was not expecting my response. He put up his hands, dropped his weapon, and turned his horse around and they galloped away.

The gun was at my feet.

I had a choice. I could bend down and pick it up, or I could leave it where it was.

I did look at it. Examined it. It was a fine piece of craftsmanship. It was smooth and looked like it would be able to take care of itself. Strange thoughts coming from me. What did I know about whether something could take care of itself or not? Surely that was a property of creatures, not objects.

"Hey," I called to the man, still running. "Come back. I'm not going to hurt you."

I did pick up the gun.

But I smashed it on a rock, just like I did with the other weapons. It didn't break up right away. I had to slam it against the rock several times until it finally broke into two pieces.

"And you aren't going to hurt me," I said.

The sound of the disintegrating gun must have stopped him. He turned around and looked my way. I couldn't see his features in the dim early morning light, but I did see that he was a short and pudgy man. I heard him huffing and puffing, trying to get air. Clearly not used to running.

He stood a distance away. "That was an expensive gun," he said.

"Not my problem," I said. "If you point it at someone, you shouldn't be surprised by the reaction you get."

He hesitated. "Fair enough."

"Is there something about guns," I asked, "around here? Everywhere I go, people are pointing guns at me."

"They're probably scared of you."

"Nothing to be scared of."

"I seen you on TV."

"Yes, I heard I'm a star. A reluctant one."

"They call you Cal?"

I nodded. "What's your name?"

"Victor," he said.

"You feel like a winner, Victor?"

"Think I haven't heard that one before?"

I laughed. He seemed like an okay guy. Maybe he was afraid of me. Maybe that was the best reaction to me. Maybe I needed to be feared. After all, I was not something natural. I was a strange hybrid.

"I'm pretty hungry," I said.

"Okay."

"You got a place near here?"

He nodded. "But I'm not going to take you there."

For a brief fleeting instant I regretted destroying the gun. It suddenly felt empowering to think about it in my hand, pointing it at Victor and making him get me some food.

"You were going to shoot me."

"A warning shot. That's all. I didn't want to kill."

I believed him, but that didn't help me get any food. I was actually beginning to get weak from the lack of food.

"Can you at least tell me where I am?"

He hesitated, then shrugged. The sky was lightening and I saw that he was a bearded fellow. He wore a light jacket and jeans. His hair was all messed up. I thought maybe he had been some rich rancher, now I saw that if he was, he was probably an eccentric one. Or maybe he worked for a rich rancher.

"Okay, Victor," I said. "You got your suspicions. I get it. Maybe this is where we part ways and bid good luck to each other."

I backed away from him. Slowly. I adopted a kind of hang dog look, like I was so depressed I might kill myself.

I was trying to appeal to the guy's humanity. Or, at least, discover if he had any.

He took a step back from me.

That was another thing. People were always stepping back from me. It was beginning to give me a feeling that I was not worth talking to or being around.

I shook my head at Victor. "You're a cruel man," I said.

I backed away and was preparing to turn, when he held up his hand.

"Wait," he said.

I stopped. Tried not to look like I was happy to hear his next words.

"I know a guy."

"Yeah."

"He has a show."

A show. I didn't know what that meant. I waited. Victor saw I was puzzled.

"Well, not a show, exactly. More like a—um, carnival I guess you would call it."

"Spit it out, Victor."

"He travels around. He has people who—well, they aren't exactly *right*. He's got twins that are joined together. He's got really small people. People with horns in their heads. That kind of thing."

"You're talking about a freak show, Victor."

He nodded.

And there it was. I had finally found my calling.

"What are you saying, Victor?"

"He has security. Good security. And he's well off. He makes a lot of money going from town to town and letting people look at the freaks." He turned a shade of red. "I mean, the special people. You would be safe with him."

"That's the best you can come up with for me?"

He shrugged again. "I don't have a lot of resources," he said.

"You have a gun."

"Had. I found that one, anyway. I can't afford a gun."

"This guy," I said, "he's around here?"

"I'll take you to him."

"I don't want to be a freak," I said. "I don't want to be in a freak show."

"What else can you do in this world? You said yourself people are always pointing guns at you. No one tries to shoot a performer in a show."

He had a point. I raised my chin. Must have looked like I was thinking about it, which I was. Victor noticed.

"He'll feed you, man," he said. "All the food you want. And he'll protect you."

"From people like you, right?"

Victor laughed. It was short and shocking, more like a snort. It made me flinch. "You make it sound like it's a bad thing," he said. You got something. People will want to see it, I guarantee you. You can live out here, in the wild, with people trying to hunt you down, or you can live with his protection."

Up to that moment, I had felt like I had a chance at being something important. Why not?

But now it felt different. The lightening sky was not a prelude to a better life. I didn't feel as though illumination was forthcoming and I would suddenly find myself happy. I was beginning to understand that my hybrid form was not going to allow that, no matter what nature was ready to offer in the way of warm feelings.

"Victor," I said, "you talk a good game, but I don't want to be a freak. I'd rather die."

I didn't know I was going to say that, but as soon as I

did say it, it felt exactly right. It felt like the answer to all my problems.

"No, Cal," said Victor. "You don't want to believe that."

"But I do," I said. "The next person that holds a gun up to me, I'm not going to try to attack them or evade them or do anything that would cause them to miss. I'm just going to accept my fate."

Victor looked down at the ground and kicked at the dust. "You sure?" he asked.

"I'm sure," I said.

"Okay, then," he said.

He reached behind himself and pulled out a gun. *Another* damned gun. They were everywhere and I was running into all of them, somehow.

I didn't care. I was prepared to die. "Make it quick," I said, and stretched my arms out wide to give him a good target on my chest.

SEVENTEEN

Victor laughed. "You're crazy, man," he said.

My arms were still stretched out. I felt like I was grabbing hunks of sky preparatory to moving up up up to heaven. Or whatever was above the blue. I was just waiting for the bullet to punch through me.

"Here," said Victor. He turned the gun around in his hands so the handle was toward me. "It's yours." He stood in front of me.

"I don't want a gun," I said. "What would I do with it?"

"We're a gun culture," he said. "Everyone has one. Or should. You, too. You should have a gun. Protection. You carry a gun long enough, and you feel invincible. You can go anywhere, do anything."

"I already go anywhere," I said.

"In fear. You don't want that. You don't want to be afraid."

I had already smashed some firearms. I was prepared to smash this one too.

"At least shoot it," he said. "At least once."

"You think if I shoot it, I'll grow to love it?"

"Works for most people," he said. He had a sly smile on his face, like he was passing on incredible wisdom. I wasn't buying any of it. He was crazy, just like most of the people I had met so far. I was starting to think that my best course of action at this point was to get to know some horses. Maybe run with a few wild herds. Was that possible? I knew horses wouldn't have guns. They wouldn't try to kill me.

"What do you want me to shoot at?" I asked.

Victor looked around. "There's a saguaro," he said, pointing to a tall cactus about 50 yards away with several arms going up its sides. "Let's see what you got in you."

"That cactus never did anything to me."

"Man," said Victor, "you are really a strange dude."

"You only just noticed?"

"Maybe you need to find a nice female, you know."

"If you're talking about what I think you're talking about," I said, "that ship has sailed."

He looked puzzled, then shrugged. "Considering your anatomy, there must be some strange plumbing going on with you," he said.

"Exactly," I said. "Everything about me is strange."

I lifted the weapon up so my arm was extended straight toward the saguaro. I lined up as best I could, then tried to hold the gun as steady as possible. It felt like an odd piece of fruit in my hand. The handle was slightly soft, like it was covered in some yielding material. Maybe to make it feel more comfortable? That was thoughtful of the manufacturers. Don't want to feel fatigued when sending bullets into other beings. Take all the fun out of it, I was sure.

I pulled the trigger.

The air around me exploded.

I gasped.

A hole bloomed in the saguaro near where one of the branches went out from the side and curved up toward the sky.

Victor cheered.

I felt sick. Had I really just harmed that saguaro?

I had.

I pulled the trigger again. Then several more times.

I put more holes in the cactus. Birds rose up from the desert floor. They screeched their protest. Too much noise. I didn't like the noise either. It made my ears ring. And the recoil was hurting my arm. I wanted to drop the weapon.

But I didn't.

I looked at Victor, who was off to the side of me. He turned and looked at me, a big grin on his face.

"You're a good shot," he said. "Where'd you learn that?"

"I didn't," I said.

"A natural, then. That's cool."

"It doesn't feel cool," I said.

His expression changed from general joy to a dark pain in an instant. "Man," he said, "you are the biggest buzz kill I've ever seen."

I gave him back the gun.

"Thanks," I said, "but no thanks."

"You can't depend on your mythical status for protection, man," he said. "People will kill anything. It doesn't matter if you're the only thing like you. Might even make it worse for you. Some guys, they'd be happy to have your head and chest hanging up on their wall."

"I'll take my chances," I said. "Maybe when I die I go back to where I belong. Ever think of that?"

"I just met you," he said. "I've never thought anything about you. Why would I?"

Now I had a grin on my face. "That's funny, Victor. Can I give you a lift anywhere?"

"Which way you going?"

I pointed away from the sun. "The hills look inviting over there."

"You'll run into Santa Fe."

"That a nice place?"

 ## Reminded of my power

"Nice enough. Probably lots of artists that would want to paint you there. Maybe want to make sculptures of you. You could make a good living as a model."

"Doesn't sound half bad," I said.

"I could introduce you around."

"You know some artists?"

"A few."

I had a sense that he was lying. That he had been lying since he met me. "There is no traveling carnival," I said. "Is there?"

He hesitated for a split second, probably trying to decide if he should keep up the story or let it go.

"No, man," he said. "I was putting one over on you."

"Why?"

"You got this—power. You don't even know it. Maybe because you're made from myth—I don't know for sure. But I wanted to make up a story. Give you a myth right back, you know?"

I didn't.

"I half want to capture you and keep you. And I half want to let you go. Let you have your wild nature. Not sure which one I should do."

I put out my hand. "You don't seem like such a bad guy. Hop on my back. We'll get to Santa Fe together."

I could see he didn't want to. Or, at least, I thought he didn't. I was having trouble reading people's faces and intentions. They were all so reserved. It was like they didn't want to reveal themselves to anyone, most especially me. Maybe because they didn't know how to understand me?

Well, we were all in the same boat. I didn't know how to understand me either.

I was completely surprised when he took my hand and I lifted him off the ground and he swung his leg up and over and ended up on my back.

"Santa Fe it is," he said.

That was about the time I heard the helicopters. He heard them too. We both looked up. Three of them came over the horizon toward us.

"This doesn't look good," he said.

I couldn't disagree.

EIGHTEEN

Victor kicked my sides with his heels.

"Hey," I said, but I'm not sure he heard me over the sound of the helicopters. They tore up the air with their roaring.

He kicked me again. I didn't want to go—there was no where to run, not really—but instinct seemed to take over and I jumped forward and kept going at a good clip. Not exactly galloping, but not trotting either.

"Fuck," he said. "You're a goddam *horse*. Get going." Then he really dug in with his heels.

I twisted around and slapped him across the face. Not hard, because the angle was wrong and I couldn't get much power behind my hand, but enough to let him know his actions were not appreciated.

"Stop doing that," I said.

He was momentarily silent, then spoke up, trying to be louder than the choppers.

"They're after you. You can't let them catch you."

"Who?" I asked. "Who's after me?"

I increased my speed to a gallop. The three choppers, which had arrived in tight formation, now distanced themselves from each other. One went forward, and one remained back. I was trotting over mostly scrubland, a few bushes and trees here and there. Some cactus. Scree covered the ground and I was afraid of slipping and falling, but my hoofs seemed to be doing the trick of keeping me upright.

The helicopter above me descended.

I heard a voice.

"Halt. Now. This is the federal government. You need to stop now or we will take action against you."

I kept going.

"Don't stop," said Victor. He had his arms around my chest and his voice was tinged with fear. A lot of fear.

"I won't."

From above, the voice on loudspeaker. "This is your last chance."

Victor released one hand from around me and pointed forward. "Looks like a safe place," he said.

I looked forward, but didn't see anything I would call a safe place.

"What?" I asked.

But before he could answer, I saw it. A church.

"Sanctuary," he said.

"Are you serious?"

"What choice do you have?"

The church was a small chapel, as far as I could tell. It was no bigger than a modest house and had a correspondingly modest wooden cross on the top.

The helicopter descended even further, so that it was no more than twenty feet above me.

"They're going to drop a net on us," said Victor, who was looking up.

"What should I do?" I asked.

"Do you have a fourth gear?" he asked.

"I don't know."

"Well, we're about to find out. When I tell you, pour on the speed. Try to go as fast as you possibly can."

"Got it," I said.

I pounded the ground. The chopper pounded the air. My hearts were going like crazy. My lungs grabbed air as fast as they could. My windup burned. I inhaled dust and heat. I was not sure I could do what Victor wanted.

"Now!" he said. "Go go go." He tried to help me by kicking my sides with renewed vigor.

Somehow—I hardly know how—I shot forward at a speed I did not know I could achieve.

100   I evade capture

Victor ducked down. I bent forward as well, copying his motion by instinct.

I felt something on my rear end, but it slipped off.

Victor cheered. "They missed!" he said.

"The net?"

"Yeah, it fell off you. Keep going."

The other helicopters began circling back. They hovered for a while, as though examining the landscape, then they shot forward, toward the church.

"They've figured out where we're going," he said.

One of the helicopters landed behind us.

The other two were descending rapidly in front of us. They would be between us and the church when they landed.

"What do I do now?" I asked, hardly able to get the words out.

"We're going to beat them," said Victor. "Just keep going."

I galloped. Hard. I felt like my hooves were breaking the ground. I had to duck, again, as we got close to the church, to keep from hitting the landing gear of the choppers.

After that, we were home free.

We got to the front of the door and we were met by—

—you guessed it. A guy with a gun.

He trained it on us and he looked like he meant business.

The two helicopters behind us were on the ground. I

heard voices as personnel poured out of the helicopters. Cries of "Halt in the name of the U.S. Government."

That's when the guy in front of the church opened fire.

NINETEEN

I lurched to the side.

The guys behind me opened fire as well. I heard shots all around me. Victor screamed.

I'm pretty sure I screamed too.

But here's the thing: none of the shot were aimed at us. At least, not on purpose. The chopper guys and the church guys were shooting at each other. We were just in the crossfire.

I went around the back of the church. There was a door there and no one guarding it.

I reached down and tried the latch. It was unlocked. I pushed the door open. It was a tight fit, but I was able to bend low and get my human part past the doorway and then I was able to squeeze the rest of me inside.

Victor remained on top of me the whole time. Pretty sure the guy was scared more than he had ever been scared in his life. I didn't blame him. He was shaking and having trouble breathing.

"We safe now?" he asked.

We were standing in the chapel. It was not a large room, but it had the solemnity of a big church. We heard shots still being fired outside, at the other end of the church, past rows of pews that were little more than unfinished planks set on blocks of wood. They looked like they had been retrieved from a constructions site.

The shooting finally stopped and the guy who had been firing stepped back into the church. He was still carrying his gun. Victor slipped off and stood next to me.

The guy stared at us.

"Well," he said. "This is a strange sight."

I nodded. "I won't argue with you."

"They coming in after you?" asked Victor.

He shook his head. "They can't. This is a church. Sanctuary, you know."

"That's what we were hoping for," I said.

The guy could not stop staring at me.

"You for real?" he asked.

"Real as you."

He considered this. "Not very reassuring," he said.

"We're looking for sanctuary from the government," I said. "They want me."

"Not surprised," he said.

"What are you doing here?" asked Victor.

"Don't ask too many questions," said the man.

"How about your name?" I asked. "I'm Cal. This is Victor."

The man was still hesitant. Still trying to fit me into some kind of slot in his world that made sense. It's not everyday you encounter a centaur. Some, like Victor, can take it in stride. Others, like the man in the church, needed more time.

"I'm Lewis," he said.

"Glad to meet you, Lewis," I said.

"Likewise."

"You got any food?" I asked.

"Did you bring any food with you?" he asked.

I shook my head. "See, it's just that I have this big body. It needs a lot of food."

"Fresh out of hay," he said.

"They going to come in after us?" asked Victor.

"I already told you," said Lewis.

"What are you doing here?" asked Victor. "You're not part of this church."

"Good guess," said Lewis.

"Like, where's the priest or whoever runs this place?"

"It's not that kind of church," said Lewis.

"Then what kind is it?"

"Just a place where people can feel safe."

That seemed like a mysterious thing to say. It didn't seem safe to be in a place where guys with guns were shooting at you. I saw tiny points of light in the walls where the sun was streaming in through bullet holes which had been punched through by projectiles from firearms. A church under siege. Seemed like the perfect metaphor for what I was going through.

"So you're okay with us being here?" asked Victor.

Lewis made a face. "You want to be here," he said,

"that's your business. Not a lot of room. Where you going to do your business? Not here. You have to go outside. Then maybe they'll nab you, yes?"

If I had human feet, I would have tapped them on the floor about then.

I heard voices coming from outside. They called for me to surrender. They were going to take care of me.

Lewis went up to the altar and retrieved gas masks and handed one each to us.

"They're going to launch tear gas now," he said. "Better put these on."

"We're a sanctuary," I said. "You just told us that."

"Only means they can't nab us when we're inside. Doesn't mean they can't try to roust us out of here."

I put the gas mask on. Victor put his on, muttering the whole time about how he made a mistake getting mixed up with me. I couldn't argue with him on that point.

We stood around for a few seconds, each of with a dark green hunk of plastic on our faces, looking like ridiculous aliens. My mask had scratches on the bug-like windows for my eyes. Everything looked like it had lines criss-crossing it.

Presently a window over the top of the front entrance shattered and a canister landed on the floor next to us. It immediately began spewing white fog.

"There it is," said Lewis.

"I'm going to give myself up," said Victor.

"Go ahead," I said. "Hope you don't get shot as you step out the front door."

That stopped him. He didn't move. Maybe from fear, maybe from an inability to see what was coming. No imagination.

I, on the other hand, could see clearly what was coming for me. I could not stay here forever. I would have to emerge from the church at some point. Then I would be captured. What would happen to me after that, I could pretty much guess. Probably some experiments. Certainly captivity. No chance for a normal life, whatever that means for a centaur in modern day America.

More canisters of tear gas came in. I picked one up and tossed it back through the broken window.

"They don't like when you do that," said Lewis.

"What do I care?" I asked.

"They'll stop soon," he said. "They like to do this every now and then."

"How long you been here?" asked Victor.

"Long enough."

Lewis had a certain reticence about his demeanor that was beginning to irritate me.

"Why are you here?" I asked.

"Listen," said Lewis through his gas mask, "the less you know, the better it is for everyone."

"I haven't found that to be the case," I said. "At least not yet."

The fog of the tear gas was dissipating.

 Mobile protection

Lewis stepped away from us and went to one of the windows at the side of the church and peered out.

"They're waiting," he said.

"For what?" I asked.

"For one of us to make a mistake."

I turned my head toward Victor. He turned to look at me. I couldn't read his expression behind the mask, and I was pretty sure mine was just as opaque to him, but I think we could both guess what the other was thinking. It went along with the rolling of eyeballs, which I'm pretty sure we were both engaging in, at least metaphorically, at that point as well.

"We're not going to make a mistake, though," said Lewis. "I've got reinforcements coming in."

"Reinforcements?" I asked.

"See, a church doesn't have to be a stationary thing."

"Okay."

"A vehicle can be designated a church. That way, you can have a mobile object that they can't touch."

"You're saying a holy bus is coming to save us."

Lewis nodded vigorously. "Isn't it great?"

"I guess so," I said.

"It was going to be just me, you know, but there's room for all of us. You need protection from the gummint, I'm there for you. The mobile home is there for us all."

"Where is it going to take us?" I asked.

Lewis shrugged. "More questions? Man, you ask a lot

of questions. Can't you just live for the now? You'll be a lot happier."

I wanted to ask him when exactly the bus or the mobile home or whatever it was was going to arrive, but he seemed to be getting a little twitchy and I didn't want to rile him up.

The air looked like it was mostly clear at that point. Lewis lifted his mask and sniffed.

"Seems okay," he said.

Victor and I lifted our masks as well. The air was acrid and I felt some burning around my eyes, but it was tolerable.

Or so I thought.

Victor began convulsing. He fell to the floor and was shaking so bad I thought he was going to injure himself.

"What's going on?" asked Lewis. "What's wrong with him?"

"I don't know," I said. "He's having a seizure."

"What the fuck," said Lewis. "I don't need this. Make him stop."

"I can't," I said.

Lewis raised his weapon. The motion was so familiar to me by then that it felt like the accompaniment to a song I had heard my whole life. An aria of firearms. An ode to force.

He extended his arm its full length so that the end of the barrel was no more than a couple of feet from my chest.

"Make him stop now," he said. "Or you're dead. Mythical beast or not, you're out of this world in five. Four. Three. Two."

TWENTY

He never got to one because I just started laughing at him. I bent back and the laughter was so loud it filled the church from end to end and side to side and snaked into every corner and every crack in the wood.

Lewis blinked.

"What's wrong with you?" he asked.

I kept laughing. Must have been a strange sight, a horse with a man's body, laughing like crazy.

"Now I have two crazies on my hands," he said.

Victor's mouth was leaking saliva. It had turned into foam. He had stopped convulsing quite so violently, but was still not right.

I stopped laughing and looked at Lewis. "We need to get Victor some medical help. Go talk to the guys outside. Get a doctor in here."

"You go talk to them," said Lewis.

I looked down the aisle to the door at the other end of the church. If I stuck my head out that door, was I going to be shot? I didn't think so, but I couldn't be sure. They did seem intent on using force.

As I contemplated my options, my phantom double appeared. It wasn't anything dramatic, it just eased itself through the ceiling and then dropped down slowly, rather in the way a leaf might drop from a tree to light on the grass below.

It landed next to Victor.

I was mesmerized by it. The bullet hole was still there right in the center of his head, but it was not as ugly as it had been before. In fact, it appeared that it was beginning to heal over.

"What are you staring at?" asked Lewis. His finger was getting twitchy on his gun. I really didn't like the way he kept it trained on me.

"Take it easy," I said. "Just wait a few minutes. I think something is going to happen here."

"What's going to happen."

"We're in a church, aren't we? If miracles happen any-where, they should happen in a church."

Lewis shook his head at me, like I was a lunatic. A lu-natic in close proximity to him. He stepped away from me and bumped into a pew, almost knocking it over.

I sensed I had an advantage, and took a couple of steps forward, my hooves making clomping sounds that echoed in the confines of the chapel.

My reverse phantom didn't notice me at all. This made me a little sad. Weren't we connected? I had hoped so, but apparently that hope was not shared.

The double went down on his knees. He had no arms. Just a human body from the feet to the waist, then a horse head beyond that. The mane was fluffy and wild, like it had been in the wind. The eyes had crusty deposits around the edges. I envied the mouth. So large. It could take in all kinds of food. Probably only needed to eat a couple of small meals a day to get enough sustenance for the slight body it had to nourish. Hell, it was only legs, really, below the horse part. A simple thing to feed, that.

The head motioned toward me, nodding in the air, like horses do.

I wasn't sure what to do.

I walked over to Victor and stood beside my phantom, who kept indicating with his head, looking first at me, then at Victor.

Lewis was mesmerized. I felt his eyes on me.

"You got some power?" he asked.

"I got something," I said.

My double leaned close to me—

—and slipped through the space between us, making itself small and big at the same time, and then it was congruent with me and I was suddenly two. A man and a horse.

I knew what to do.

I put my hands on Victor. I felt him, his presence, and yet I also felt his shadow self. He existed in two places that were separated by nothing.

His fits stopped.

"Get something to wipe his mouth," I said to Lewis, hearing the words and saying the words and observing the words. All at the same time.

Lewis bolted from the scene and disappeared.

I regret my fate  111

I had a floaty feeling in my heart. I felt as though I was in at least two places, possibly more. I was conscious of being on my feet, and conscious, as well, of being on four hooves.

Victor sighed. His arms, at his sides, were motionless, as though he was sleeping. His eyes were closed, but I saw the bulge in his eyelids from his eyeball going in circles and spirals like crazy.

Then he sat up, like a spring.

Lewis returned with a cloth. I took it and put it on Victor's mouth, but he opened his eyes and took the cloth himself.

Then everything whirled away from me. I felt myself pull out of the amalgamation we had. My phantom rose back up to the ceiling. I was a man's upper half stuck on a horse's lower half again.

I cried out. I reached up to the phantom, who was now melting through the ceiling again. I watched as the horse head went through first, then the human part and finally the feet, popping to the other side like a vegetable disappearing into boiling broth on a stove.

"Hey," said Lewis. "You fixed the poor guy."

Victor looked apologetic as he wiped his mouth with the rag Lewis had brought him.

"You have epilepsy?" I asked him.

He nodded. "Haven't had a problem for a while. My medication helps."

"You maybe forget to take it or something?"

He seemed thoughtful, thinking back. "Maybe," he said.

"Probably stress can trigger it," said Lewis.

Victor looked at him. "What do I have to be stressed about?" he asked with a perfectly straight face.

Lewis saw the humor, I think. He laughed, at least. Or maybe it was a chuckle.

"This guy," he said, motioning toward me with his gun, "knew what to do. A laying on of hands. Like a freaking god or something."

"That right?" asked Victor.

"Well," I said, "I am a mythical creature, after all." I didn't tell them about the double, the phantom that did the work.

I was going to. I wanted to. But something inside me suggested it was not the best thing to do. People had a limit to what they could assimilate of the fantastic.

Or so I thought.

"What say we break out of here," said Victor. "Get you some food."

"There's still the feds outside," I said.

"They don't want to kill you," said Victor.

"How do you know?"

"You're of no value to them dead."

"That's not much to go on."

"I'm willing," said Victor.

"So am I," said Lewis. "Take me with you."

I looked at Lewis. He had lowered his gun. That was a good sign.

"You never told us your story," I said. "Why are you here in this church? All alone. What do you need sanctuary from?"

Victor stood up and dusted himself off. He was completely normal again. Was I a miracle worker? Could it be possible?

Lewis looked at me then back to Victor. I won't say he had shifty eyes, because that sounds ridiculously melodramatic, but I will say he gave me some pause. I suddenly felt like he was more dangerous than he had been with his gun pointed at me.

"This is my church," he said. "I have squatter's rights."

I wasn't sure what that meant, but I didn't press the point.

"Just asking what brought you here," said Victor.

Lewis looked at my back side. "There's room for both of us on him," he said to Victor. "You and me."

"That's not the point," I said. "We aren't going to travel with someone unless we know who they are."

"Listen," said Lewis, "I've got the gun. You guys have to listen to me."

I saw the logic, but he wasn't even holding the gun on us. Too tired? Maybe the gun was too heavy. Or maybe he wasn't really a gun-toting kind of guy.

"Just tell us your story," said Victor.

Lewis looked like he was going to cry, which was certainly surprising.

"I got problems, man," he said.

"We guessed that," I said. "Tell us what they are. Or at least some of them. Don't go overboard or anything."

That made him laugh, which relaxed all of us.

But it didn't last because at that moment guys broke into the church from both ends at the same time. The doors flew open with a crash, and men with assault rifles and wearing heavy boots, helmets, and armor burst into the church, coming at us from both directions.

TWENTY-ONE

Lewis dropped his weapon. It hit the ground. We heard orders to lie on the ground.

"I can't," I said.

They repeated the orders. Lewis and Victor went down. I struggled to find room to lie on my side, but it was a tight fit, what with the pews and the altar and all.

"This is a sanctuary," said Lewis. "You can't break into here."

A female voice from the front entrance. "I gave permission," she said.

We looked up. A woman in flowing robes approached us.

"Who is that?" I whispered.

"The minister," said Lewis. "She said I could stay here."

"I think she's changed her mind," I said.

"No shit, Sherlock," said Lewis.

The minister pointed at me. Not with a firearm, thank goodness, but with determination, which I wasn't sure was much better.

"That one," she said firmly. "That's the one. Take him out."

An instant later all of the invaders of what was once a sanctuary trained their weapons on me.

Once again, I was prepared to die.

But, once again, it was premature.

Lewis and Victor, both on the floor, looked up at me.

"Stay down, guys," I said.

I was on my knees at that point, trying to obey the orders by the gun-toters, but now I was struggling to get up. I reasoned that if they had wanted to kill me, they would already have done so.

Since I was still alive, it meant something else was going on.

I got up off my knees.

The minister put up her arm and spread her hand. The guns dropped from their aim at me, which was a relief. I was still not used to having guns pointed at me. I hoped I never would be.

The minister strode up to me. She was a vision, I'll give her that. The robes, even when she stopped, moved like they were in a slow and languid wind. Her hair even moved like that.

"I didn't mean to cause any trouble," I said.

"You have no business here," she said. "This is a place for *people*."

"Doesn't your compassion extend to half people?" I asked.

She stared at me. We locked eyes. We remained like that for some time, each of us trying to see into the depths of the soul of the other. I wasn't even sure I had a soul. Or, to put it more accurately, I wasn't sure I had an *intact* soul. It might have been a hybrid, or even something created for all I knew. Her soul, on the other hand, was there, for sure. But it was damaged. As though she had been hurt herself in the past.

"I own horses," she said.

"Okay."

"And I have a flock. My congregation."

"Yippee."

"You are neither. I don't know where you came from, but you can't stay here. It's polluting my realm."

"I can't go outside," I said. "They'll shoot me."

"Don't be so dramatic. They don't want to shoot you."

"You haven't been following the news, I see."

She turned to the troopers. "Any of you want to shoot this centaur?" she asked.

No answer.

"Come on," she said loudly, "tell me yes or no. Do you want to shoot this abomination of nature?"

I didn't care for that last phrase. I was an anomaly, to

be sure, but abomination was going too far in my estimation. A prelude to making me expendable.

I coughed and cleared my throat, making it clear I objected to her characterization.

She turned to me. "What?"

"The abomination reference. It's a bit extreme."

She rolled her eyes. "Okay," she said to the assembled gun wielders. "I'll put it a little differently. Do any of you want to shoot—" she turned to me with a questioning look.

"Cal," I said. "The name's Cal."

"Cal," she said loudly so my name careened off the ceiling and the walls and repeated a couple of times before dying on the air.

Again a short silence, but this time it ended with a few murmurs of dissent.

"Louder," said the minister.

"No!" said a few of them in unison.

"There," she said. "You see? You're safe. Now get out of here."

I sniffed the air.

"Go, go," she said. "The great outdoors await you."

I suppose ministers, those who profess to know a little something of faith and the holy spirit, can be assholes just like anyone else, but it was still a bit of a shock.

"It would be nice if I had some food to take on my journey," I said.

"Food?" She laughed. Like I had asked for something impossible.

"I'm really hungry. I think my companions are too."

"Yup," said Victor from the floor.

"Me too," said Lewis.

"Do you know I was having a good time at home?" she asked.

I didn't, but chose not to answer her question.

"Found a free channel that was broadcasting non-stop episodes of *Zombietown USA*. It's my favorite show. They have a Jesus figure in it. He might be a zombie and he might not. We never know. That's what makes it so compelling. He does miracles, but you don't know if his miracles are God-like or just because of him being a zombie."

I nodded. "Sounds good."

"It is. You haven't seen it?"

I shook my head.

"You should. It's worth it. Anyway, like I was saying, this is my day off. I needed some relaxation, then—" she lifted up her hands again, as though pushing a balloon to the ceiling, and spun around and I swear, the robes started that dance again, and then she stopped.

"This. You. Messing up my day."

"Didn't mean to."

"So, anyway, here's the deal. I don't want them to shoot you. It's *wrong*. On so many levels. Also, if they shoot you here, I'll have to arrange for the cleanup and removal of your body. Yuck. But you need to get out. Now. Out out out."

She certainly left no room for debate. But I tried anyway.

"Let me offer a counter proposal," I said.

Her face darkened. Evidently she was not used to people arguing with her. She had God on her side. Maybe that's what made her just the teeniest bit of a control freak. Maybe.

"I'm listening," she said. "For about two seconds."

"Baptize me."

Here she doubled over and laughed and laughed. "You have got to be kidding."

"I don't want to meet my maker without being saved."

"Who is your maker?"

"God, maybe. Or some kid with a biology degree and a cruel streak. Or some government experiment gone wrong. Or a bunch of dreams linked in a Jungian archetypal manifestation project. Who knows? I don't. And neither do you. So just for the sake of safety, baptize me."

She wanted to say no. I could tell. It was on her lips. She was ready.

But then she softened. She maybe saw the wisdom of what I was saying. Or the absurdity. And she seemed to like the idea of absurd.

"You know there's nothing that says I have to."

"I know," I said, "but I'm appealing to your sense of right and wrong."

She didn't like that, either, but she let it go. I was flattering her, after all.

 # A dramatic entrance

"I've never baptized a half man," she said.

"Do a half ceremony, then," I said.

She laughed again. I couldn't tell if it was a bitter laugh or a joyous one. But I knew something had changed.

"Here's what I'll do," she said. "First I'll get you some food. Then I'll consider your proposal."

"That's all I ask," I said.

She turned from me and called to the assembled feds. "Stand down," she said. "This is over, for now."

Hardly had the words left her lips, than the walls began to tremble.

I felt a rumbling under my feet. Victor and Lewis felt it too. So did the minister. We all looked up. The ceiling was vibrating and dust was falling off of it, staining the air.

Then the side wall collapsed, crashing down around us. Splintered wood everywhere, snapping and cracking and puncturing the air. Everyone scattered to the opposite wall but it was too late.

The armored vehicle that had broken down the wall, all green and huge and determined and menacing, advanced into the building, flattening pews as it relentlessly came toward me.

TWENTY-TWO

At least it wasn't a gun.

But it was still a weapon, and I was still in danger.

Maybe I should have thought only of myself. After all,

I was the obvious target. Instead, I reached down and helped Victor and Lewis to their feet.

The armed guys turned their weapons on the armored vehicle and began shooting. Bullets bounced off the thing and careened around the church, what was left of it.

The minister was brave, I'll give her that.

She strode to a spot in front of the armored vehicle. I heard shouts that the shooting should stop. It did. The shooters still held their weapons at the ready, but stopped firing.

The minister put up her hands, halting the armored vehicle.

I have to say, that really impressed me. I let out a whoop, hardly believing the syllable came from my mouth. Victor and Lewis joined, cheering her.

"I've always been scared of her," said Lewis, "but I've always known she was completely baddass."

"You destroyed my church," said the minister. "You're going to hear from God about this. And our lawyers."

I thought that was funny, and I laughed.

Then a crackling sound snapped the air. A voice came over a loudspeaker, evidently from the armored vehicle.

"Sorry for the dramatic entrance. We've already deposited enough funds into your bank account to repair the damage to your church. With a generous bonus for the inconvenience, which you can use for a general spruce up of the property and building. That cross could use a little polishing."

I make a stand

The minister, still with her robes flowing, and still with her hands up, blinked.

"Um," she said. "Thank you. I think."

"We're here for Cal. The centaur."

That was my cue. "Hell no," I said. "I won't go."

I reasoned that they were crazy. At least as crazy as anyone else I had met up to that point, and maybe a little bit more. I was enjoying my sanctuary in the church. It paradoxically offered me some freedom. Freedom to be more me. Freedom to relax.

Victor nudged me. "What are you doing?" he asked. "There's your chance. Take it."

Lewis nodded vigorously. "Take it, man," he said. "If it was me, I'd go like that." He snapped his fingers.

Everyone turned to him. Some of the weapons turned and pointed at him.

He held up his hands. "I'm just a sanctuary seeker," he said. "No trouble, please."

"He's right," said the minister. "Leave him alone. He thinks the government is oppressing him because he's an alien from another planet. He's harmless."

I blinked. "Is that true?" I whispered to Lewis.

"Yup," he said. "I'm from another galaxy, actually. The government wants to dissect me, but I won't let them. She sees my side of things and won't turn me over. She also invited nice people to come talk to me a couple of times a week. We discuss my past, the memories of my home world. It's nice."

Victor and I looked at each other with knowing glances. We sure felt superior in that moment.

"We'll double the deposit," said the loudspeaker. "Hand over the centaur and you can build another church. One that you will be proud of."

The minister hesitated. "We're already proud of this one," she said. But she didn't sound convincing. Not at all.

"There," said the loudspeaker. "Doubled. Are there any other terms of agreement you would like to add to the arrangement?"

"I wouldn't mind us buying the adjoining property," said the minister.

A few seconds of silence while she auctioned me off. I wasn't happy about it, but did I mention she was formidable? I didn't want to object too strenuously, although I did speak up. "I could be a real attraction," I said to her. "People would come from miles around to see me. From the entire world. You could end up with a mega church."

That sounded reasonable, but even as I said it, I sensed she was not going to go for it.

Victor groaned. "Nooooooo," he said. "That's not what she wants. Don't you know anything about people?"

I had to admit that I did not. The minister looked me up and down, as though calculating the consequences of what I just said.

Then she dismissed me with a wave of her flowing hand.

She addressed the armored vehicle. "Done," she said. "He's all yours."

"Wait a minute," I said. "I didn't agree to this."

I moved to get out the back way, through the door I had used to enter the church.

The minister came over to me.

Did I mention she had some kind of strange power? Well, she did. I froze, waiting for her.

"Look," she said, "I know you hoped for safety here, but I can't have you in my church. It's a mess, in case you haven't noticed, all because of you."

"And you got a good deal out of selling me."

"Don't be bitter. These guys seem very reasonable."

"To you."

"To me. But I have a feeling about this. I know people. They will take care of you."

She was diabolical, no doubt about it. But the way she spoke, and her mannerisms, they were so mild and understanding and, well, *nice*, that I couldn't refuse her.

"What about the guys with guns?" I asked.

"I'll take care of them."

"I'm still hungry," I said.

"They'll feed you."

"How do you know?"

"I know that sustenance and abundance come from faith. You should have more faith."

Was she right? She could have been. I looked past her to Victor and Lewis. They were huddled together. Scared?

I didn't think so. They seemed to be cheering me on in their quiet way. Their thumbs were raised above their fists, like long-necked creatures tilting their heads to the stars.

The gun bearers behind them were getting tired. A lot of them had dropped the butts of their weapons to the floor and were leaning on them for support.

So many people interested in me. It was a bit overwhelming and I really didn't know what decision I should make. That's the funny thing. That I thought I had a choice.

A door swung open on the side of the armored vehicle, making a seam of light at the top. The door eased down slowly toward the floor, crushing a pew as it went, until it became a ramp. It had slats across its width, evidently to help my hooves navigate its length.

I raised my voice. "Can I bring my friend with me?"

"Who's your friend?" asked the loudspeaker.

I pointed to Victor. "That guy," I said.

"Sure," said the loudspeaker.

"How about it?" I asked Victor.

"Hell yes," he said.

"Okay, then," I said.

The minister looked relieved. "It's the best thing for all of us," she said.

I didn't care for her tone at that moment. She didn't know what was best for anyone, let alone for me. But I didn't press the point. Why rock the boat now?

"Lewis?" I asked. "You want to come too?"

He shook his head. "This is home for me. For now. I don't want to go. I'll help rebuild."

The minister spread her hands. She was good at that. Must have practiced.

"There," she said. "You see? Everyone knows what is best."

I licked my lips and stepped forward. Victor came up beside me. The guys with guns all retreated from us.

"You sure about this?" asked Victor.

At the other end of the ramp, I saw only a dark space. No person made themselves visible. I could not see anything except a dark shadow, which seemed to be boiling with portent and possible doom.

"Not at all," I said to Victor. "Not even close."

TWENTY-THREE

I shouldn't have been afraid.

Easy to say now, but at the time I was so scared I couldn't hold my piss and I let loose with a gushing stream that splashed on the floor of the church and sprayed moisture out quite extensively.

The minister jumped back. "Oh," she said, "that's very nice."

"Sorry," I said. "Couldn't hold it."

"Still learning the plumbing?" she asked.

I didn't want to let her know I was afraid, so I just agreed with her.

"Well, learn it somewhere else," she said, clearly disgusted with me.

"I don't know why I'm here," I said. "I don't know how I got to this planet. This world. You can't blame me for just being who I am."

I hoped she might soften, a little, but she didn't. Victor grabbed my arm. "Come on," he said. "We going to go or aren't we?"

The ramp going up to the armored vehicle was narrower than I would have liked. It would have been plenty wide for me if I was just a man, but I was more than a man, so there you are. I stepped on it gingerly. Victor went around me and stepped up onto it and just about sprinted into the interior and disappeared in the darkness.

"You better be nice people," I said to the dark doorway in front of me.

No answer.

"Victor?" I asked. "Everything okay in there?"

"Yes," he said. "Just come on it. Everyone's real nice."

That gave me some confidence. I stepped forward. The ramp was slippery. One of my hooves scuttled out from under me and I had to regain my balance for a moment.

"On my way," I said a little shakily.

Even before I was all the way in, the ramp began raising up. I felt my rear end go up and that got me going even quicker.

The interior of the vehicle was very dark. I stepped off

the ramp, it kept going up until it closed and latched. Then I felt the vehicle back up.

"Where's the driver?" I asked.

I felt the wheels crunch over the debris of the broken wall. We moved slowly, but relentlessly. As my eyes grew accustomed to the darkness, I could make out some features. There was a narrow window at the front and the back. The room I was in was quite cramped, especially for me. I had to keep my head bent at an angle to not hit the ceiling.

"There's no one here," said Victor. I could see his teeth in the murky gray of the air inside the vehicle. He was grinning wide.

"What?"

"It's a driverless vehicle."

"But we heard people. On the loudspeaker."

Victor laughed. "Remote personnel. They must have cameras on the outside."

"Dammit," I said. "I wanted to talk to my rescuers. If they are rescuers. You think we've been kidnapped?"

"How the hell would I know? I just didn't want to wait around those trigger happy freaks at the church."

I shuffled closer to one of the windows. I felt the vehicle picking up speed. I looked through the narrow glass and saw desert scenes recede from me, punctuated with long tire tracks. Our tire tracks.

"Victor," I said, "I think I might have made a mistake. Should have counted on the sanctuary of the church."

Victor shook his head. "No way, man, this was the only way out. The only way to *survive.*"

I had an urge to sit down. My human part wanted to separate from my horse part and find a comfortable chair and lower my posterior into it. A strange sensation, feeling as though I had to cut or break myself in two.

My horse part had no such urges. It only wanted food. Always and forever, it was going to want to be fed.

The vehicle increased its speed. We were moving far faster than I thought it was possible for the operators to keep track of.

"I'm going to look around," said Victor.

"You do that," I said, dejection coloring my words.

"Now don't be that way," said Victor. "We're in a safe vehicle here. No one's going to attack us. We're being taken care of. The operators don't want to hurt us."

"You're making a lot of assumptions," I said.

He shrugged.

"I could see an argument for me not being in danger, but I'm a prize. You, on the other hand, might just be expendable."

It was a cruel thing to say. Unnecessary, really, but I was in a pissy mood and I didn't much care about Victor at that moment.

"You make a good point," said Victor. "But I've got it all planned out. When we get to where we're going, if things look bad for me, I'm going to take you hostage."

130 ⚹ I face a firearm again

He said it with such a straight face and a serious tone that for a second I wasn't sure if he was kidding or not.

Then I decided he was pranking me and I laughed. He didn't join in.

"I could kick you to death without even breaking a sweat," I said.

He bent down, lifted up the cuff of his pant, and reached under and pulled a gun out of a holster strapped to his leg.

"I got firepower," he said. He pointed the gun at me.

Oh, for the love of everything equine, there was the symbol of everything, staring me in the face once more: a firearm.

"I thought I wrecked your gun," I said.

"I always carry a spare." He grinned.

Of course.

"Isn't it commonly agreed that one should not point a weapon unless one is prepared to use it?" I asked.

"I'm ready. Like I said, if the situation demands it, I'm up for it."

As I have indicated, the space we shared was very small. We were being jostled up and down as we went. My hooves were rattling against the floor. Victor's gun, which he was brandishing in my direction with what I thought was cavalier abandon, displayed a blurred barrel as it got bumped around with everything else.

If felt like this was a test of our alliance, such as it was.

"You won't shoot me now," I said.

"I wouldn't bet my life on that," he said.

"Let me ask you a question," I said.

"Go ahead."

"What is it with all the guns? Ever since I've arrived, there's been nothing but guns guns guns. It's getting a little tiresome."

"If I have to explain it, you'll never get it," he said.

That seemed like a non answer, but I didn't challenge him on it. I didn't have the energy.

Instead, I shuffled to the front of the vehicle, and looked out the window there. The landscape came at me with frightening speed. We mostly traversed level ground, but occasionally we hit some bumps. Far off in the distance, I thought I saw the edge of a ravine. It looked like there was nothing but empty space beyond it.

I thought that couldn't be the case, but as time went on, it became clear we were heading for danger.

"Come over here," I said to Victor.

"You want to jump me or something?" he asked.

"Just come look at this."

My tone must have conveyed something urgent. He lowered the gun, returned it to its holster, and came and stood beside me.

The edge of the ravine was getting closer all the time. It now looked like it was less than about 500 feet distant. We would get to it in probably under a minute.

Victor stared through the window for a couple of seconds, then whistled.

"We are in deep shit," he said.

TWENTY-FOUR

"We need to jump out," I said.

Victor frantically ran his hands over the door. "I can't find a latch," he said.

I put my hand on the door. I couldn't find a door handle either.

"Hey," I said to the air, "whoever is driving this. You're taking us over a cliff. Stop. Or turn. Something."

No answer.

"You were pretty vocal when you wanted to get us into this death trap," I said. "All quiet now?"

"We're getting closer," said Victor.

"Give me your gun," I said.

"You want to shoot me?"

"Hand it over."

I must have spoken with something approaching authority, because he reached down to his leg holster and gave me the gun. Must have figured he was going to die anyway.

I took the weapon and pointed it at the door.

"Give that back," he said. "You don't know what you're doing."

He was right, but I didn't see much in the way of options. I fired two quick shots.

The sound reverberated and rang through the little enclosure. The bullets ricocheted off the door. I didn't expect that, which, in retrospect was pretty idiotic of me and probably what Victor was objecting to.

When the ringing died down, I saw Victor slumped over to one side. His chest displayed a growing circle of red around a deeply red spot about the diameter of an eye.

"Victor," I said.

But he was gone. No answer and no movement.

I didn't want to kill the guy.

I kicked at the door with my hind legs, trying to push the damn thing open, but it wouldn't budge.

I screamed at the walls. Victor's blood was seeping onto the floor and I was stepping in it.

I looked through the front window again, pushing Victor aside with no respect at all. I was frantic with panic. Couldn't get myself to calm down and work the problem. There wasn't any *time*. Not anymore.

As the cliff edge drew closer and closer, I did, finally, after what seemed like hours but was only a few seconds, see my way to some kind of peace with what was about to happen to me.

I had arrived in this world unheralded and I was going to leave in a most ignoble manner. There was a certain rightness to that. I really didn't have any cause to expect anything different.

The vehicle seemed to increase its speed. I had a short time to consider the option of closing my eyes or leaving them open all the way down. I elected to keep them open. Face my demise fully and with all faculties alert.

But just before I got to the edge, the vehicle slowed rapidly and came to a stop.

I was barely six feet from the edge. Maybe less. My hearts were going like crazy. Their pounding filled my body. I felt my blood rush through me like a thunderstorm raging. The only sound in the cabin was my own breathing, full and ragged and fairly scooping up air like it was about to disappear.

The door moved, revealing a thin line of light along the edges where it met the doorway.

It began moving down. I didn't wait for it. I hit it, hard, so it went forward and turned into the ramp that brought me into the vehicle in the first place.

I stepped outside.

The sun was low on the horizon. It would be dark soon. I stood in the soft sweet light. The ground was illuminated all fiery red and the sky was a soft blue, like it had been made by angels. Everything all around me was pure and vivid and almost painfully bright.

The loudspeaker came on.

"There's a path behind you," it said. "It leads down the ravine. Take it."

I turned, kicking up a substantial amount of dust as I did so, which got into my nose and mouth and made me cough and sneeze.

"Why should I?" I asked.

"You have no better options at this point."

"I could strike out on my own."

"You don't know where you are."

The voice had a point. I had no idea where to go. No idea if there was anyone who wouldn't shoot at me when I was out in the wilderness of this world.

"We have food," the voice said.

My ambivalence wavered.

"Victor is dead," I said. "I shot him. Accidentally."

No answer from the loudspeaker. I waited patiently. As I did so, my phantom appeared from inside the vehicle. It stood in the doorway.

"What are you doing here?" I asked it, but it had no answer for me, as I expected it would not.

It floated down from the vehicle and went right past me, not inches from my face. Its horse's head was glowing with a kind preternatural light, as though it was illuminated from within. I saw its glowing eyes with a mixture of awe and terror. Would I have had those big eyes? Would I have seen things that I wasn't now seeing? I longed for those eyes. Coveted them.

The phantom kept going. It walked to the edge of the cliff, and veered over to one side and disappeared down the path.

"Did you do that?" I asked.

"We did nothing. We're trying to assess the implications of you killing Victor."

 # Invited to a meeting

"Remember, it was a mistake. An accident. Remember that."

"Even so," said the voice.

I turned to the cliff edge. I stepped forward. It was indeed a deep ravine. I saw a river, far below. It was a thin thread of blue, almost lost in the shadows, but definitely there. Perhaps 300 feet down. The path cut through the side of the ravine.

It looked somewhat treacherous. One wrong step and I would be over the edge, falling to my death.

Which, as I thought about it, didn't seem like such an awful fate any longer. Death had its attractions, if not its rewards.

"What do you want with me?" I asked.

"Meet with us and we'll tell you," said the loudspeaker.

I didn't like the sound of that.

"You make it sound like you're asking me to a meeting voluntarily. But you brought me here. More or less against my will."

"We apologize for that."

"Doesn't sound sincere," I said.

The big wide world beckoned behind me. My tail swished in anticipation. I relished the thought of galloping free. Letting the wind be my companion. Feeling the earth push back on my flying hooves.

Instead, I was having a conversation with—

—who?

I didn't even know. Just a voice in the air.

As I was standing there on the edge, trying to decide what I should do next, the ground began to rumble.

And shake.

An earthquake? I didn't know. I stepped back from the edge.

The vehicle that brought me began to tremble, like it was shaking from fear.

I took more steps.

"What's happening?" I asked.

"Come down to us," came the voice. It suddenly sounded sinister, like it wanted to hurt me.

I decided I was not going to let it.

I turned and prepared to begin running.

But my rear legs did not grip any soil. Instead, the ground gave way, and I fell backward with my hooves flailing and my arms reaching forward and grabbing nothing but empty air.

TWENTY-FIVE

By that time I had already had a few moments where my world was falling out from under me, either metaphorically or realistically. I had also been through a few moments when I thought my life was at risk.

This time was different. It really shakes up your view of reality when the ground itself decides that it isn't going to be solid anymore.

138 Gravity asserts itself

I am more than a little ashamed to say I screamed with panic, calling for the gods to help me.

I hardly knew what gods might be available to assist me, but that didn't stop my instinctual brain from invoking them. And cursing them. I managed to get out a few lines of protest and fear, tinged with anger, before gravity took hold and grabbed my combined human and equine form and pulled me down with a might and power that any god would envy.

Gravity, after all, is an absolute law of the universe. Nothing escapes it. Certainly not me.

I saw the vehicle go over first, slipping out of view without any fuss whatsoever. I was going to be next. I worked my legs against the crumbling ground, trying to find purchase but achieving none.

As I went over the side, I was completely resigned to my fate. I hoped the end would come quickly. That I might be smashed against the rocks next to the river far below, or even crack my skull open on the way down. I yearned for such a release. Much better that than surviving the crash with massive internal injuries and lingering in pain for hours or days before expiring.

They were curious thoughts, I suppose, but they came to me without me asking for them.

I had absolutely no thought that I would be rescued.

Not even when I fell into the net that had been deployed for the purpose of saving me.

By the time I whooshed into its embrace, I had turned

in the air like a tumbling leaf and was upside down, my hands extended forward, my tail flapping in the wind, my horse legs working spasmodically against the air.

I cried out as I saw the mesh approaching me. It was suspended by two poles extending from the wall of the ravine. It strained against my weight, stretching as I fell into it. I had tried to move myself in the air just before impact, so that the weight of my equine portion would not crush my human portion, but I was not completely successful and I felt a strain at my back where fur met skin.

I cried out from the pain.

The mesh stretched and then bounced back, sending me up into the air a short distance. My stomach felt like it wanted to crawl up my throat.

I bounced for a few seconds. The mesh held me as rocks and debris rained down around me. Some of them hit me on my equine back and a few even connected with my head.

That hurt, but I didn't care, not at that moment. I was alive, and I had to work through the implications of that. I wasn't at all sure it was a good thing because now I was captive.

I tried to right myself on the mesh, but it was impossible to do so. All I managed was to get myself winded and sweaty.

That was when the mesh began moving sideways. It retracted into an opening in the side of the ravine, which I had not even noticed up to that moment.

140   I choose oblivion

Beyond the opening was a dark space. I tried to discern some details in the black air. None presented themselves. It was all darkness.

I scrambled to get out, but only managed to get my hooves tangled up in the mesh.

The mesh began slowly descending.

Once it contacted the floor and spread out, I was able to find purchase on something solid and stood up.

I felt pain throughout my body, but nothing broken as far as I could tell.

My eyes were still getting used to the dark when I saw two indistinct shapes in the distance.

I thought to charge at them, but held myself back.

The shapes resolved themselves into silhouettes of human beings. A man and a woman.

Each of them held something in their hands.

As they got closer, I saw that the objects were weapons.

I did not want to wait for what would happen next. I was done with firearms.

I turned from them and galloped back toward the opening, knowing the other side was a long drop to the ravine below.

TWENTY-SIX

Ah, but they saw the possibility of my bolting.

As I got closer to the opening, a door fell from the top and closed it off, completely blocking my exit.

They were cunning, I'll give them that. Sharp, too.

I skidded to a stop. Then, feeling my eyes ablaze with rage, I turned and glared at the two figures.

They stood in front of me. They held out plates.

Of food.

Not weapons. I had imagined those.

I breathed the air in the enclosure with some reticence, not knowing, for the moment, what was in store for me. Was I a guest? A captive? Something in between?

The plates were more than plates. They were amazing large serving platters, laden with what looked like roasted vegetables, broiled fish, mounds of rice, piles of beans, stacks of tortillas, and baked squash. The oversized plates had to be supported by two hands.

The people holding them smiled at me, the way someone who might be considering the possibility of stabbing you in the back might smile.

But I took no time to examine, greet, or fear them. My mouth was salivating. My stomachs were churning.

They stepped back, holding the platters up like bait. I walked forward, taking the bait. I was powerless to help myself.

They came to a table, where they put the platters down, then stepped back even further to make the invitation even more enticing.

The table also held a large jug of water and a regular sized glass for pouring into. They thought of everything.

I began eating. The food might have been good, it

might have been terrible. I barely tasted it I ate so fast. The bottomless pit of my hunger needed to be filled.

I chewed noisily, looking up only occasionally at the two people, who stood watching me with benign expressions.

Which raised my suspicions. They were hiding something, it seemed clear to me.

"You do this sort of thing often?" I asked.

"No," said the man.

"Because creatures like you are rare," said the woman.

She stepped forward and offered me a glass of water. I downed it. She poured me another one, and I gulped it quickly, then returned to the food.

"My name is Viola," said the woman. "This is Andy."

"Good for you," I said. They glanced at each other with a can-you-believe-this-guy? kind of look between them.

"I'd like to be social," I said, "but I'm hungry. You must have realized that, since you brought this food to me."

"We guessed," said Viola. "Do you know why you're here?"

"No," I said. "I'm guessing you two are some kind of mad scientists. You want to do experiments on me. It's a little bit sick and a little bit noble. The search for knowledge and all, but also a chance to cater to your sadistic streak, which is mostly hidden away, but which kind of needs to be attended to now and then, and horror movies aren't doing it for you anymore."

No sound from either of them.

I lose my appetite  143

"Oh come on," I said. "You're quiet because that was close to the *truth?*"

I stood there with a tortilla in my hand, smeared with guacamole and heaped with rice, beans and vegetables.

"Not exactly," said Andy.

"Glad to hear it," I said as I downed the tortilla and its accompaniments in two bites, then proceeded to build another.

"But close," said Viola.

I didn't want to hear that.

"Just eat up," said Viola. "Satisfy your hunger. Don't worry about running out. There's plenty more. We know you have to eat."

But I had suddenly lost my appetite.

"What do you mean by 'close?'" I asked.

"We do want to gain knowledge from you."

"Knowledge is overrated," I said. "Food is the only important thing in the world."

"We're wondering," said Andy.

"Yes?"

"Why did you kill Victor?"

"I told the voice," I said. "An accident." I put the tortilla down on the table.

"That's hard to believe," said Viola.

"Hard or not, it's the truth. I was trying to blast a hole through the door of your kidnapping machine. Trying to escape, you know? To gain my freedom? You do believe in freedom, right?"

"Freedom is overrated," said Andy, imitating my voice. Now I was scared.

I stepped back from both of them. My hooves clattered on the floor.

"Come on," said Viola. "Don't be so skittish. We're harmless. We want to help you."

Never trust anyone who says they want to help you. That's wisdom from a mythical creature. You can take that to the bank.

"Define help," I said.

"Well," said Viola, "first off, you're naked."

"I have fur."

"On only part of you, and fur isn't clothes."

"So what are you saying?"

"We can make you some clothes. Andy is a good sewer."

"It's true," he said. "I can make you a fine suit of clothes."

"I don't know," I said. "What's in it for you?"

"Never mind that," said Andy. "Once you have some decent clothes, the whole world will open up for you. You'll see."

They *did* look like they wanted to help. The great blue sky above only knew why. And it wasn't telling me.

"Also," said Viola, "you need weaponry. You are defenseless."

"Not defenseless," I said, perhaps a little too quickly.

"Really?" asked Andy. "Did you notice how easy it was for *us* to nab you?"

He had a point. "I've fired a gun," I said. "I don't like it."

"Not firearms," said Andy. "A bow. With arrows."

"Why? Because you have a constellation that suggests that to you?"

"Is there a better reason?" asked Viola.

They both still displayed smiles. Lots of smile. With plenty of teeth showing, like they were modeling their chewing apparatus.

"Anything else?"

"You need a career."

I snorted. Almost *sounded* like a horse for a second. "What do I need a career for?"

"Everyone needs a job," said Viola. "Without one, you don't have any purpose in life."

Okay, I was beginning to see that they were woefully lacking in imagination. Did they really think working for money was the most important thing one could do?

"I suppose you have one picked out for me."

They both nodded vigorously. Like their heads were going to get knocked off their necks from the motion.

"Do tell," I said.

"It's a surprise."

I shook my head, almost as vigorously as they nodded theirs. "No way," I said. "You have to tell me. You can't keep me in the dark. Then I'm just your plaything. Something for you to feel good about. But I'm not interested in whether you feel good about it or not. I have to look after myself."

"Hold on," said Viola, displaying her palm. She and Andy huddled behind the table, bent toward each other and whispering in each other's ear.

While they conferred, I looked over the remains of the food. I had scarfed down most of it. I had to admit Viola and Andy really were nice enough to me that I could let my guard down. They hadn't done anything to raise my suspicions yet. Well, besides kidnapping me.

They broke their huddle and looked at me.

They could hardly contain their excitement. Andy was jumping up and down, and then Viola joined him.

"We're going to make you the president of the United States," they said in unison.

TWENTY-SEVEN

The silence in the room after that statement was a palpable thing. It hung over all three of us and I'll tell you the truth, I wish they had been joking, but I could tell they weren't.

"I was hoping I wasn't trapped with crazy people," I said. "Looks like I was dead wrong."

"Now don't be that way," said Viola. "We have a plan."

"A plan that, when fulfilled, makes me president?"

They both nodded.

"You're forgetting Victor's death. A guy who shoots someone dead won't be president."

"That's what *we* thought," said Viola.

"At first," said Andy.

"Then we thought about it some more and decided it was going to be your test," said Viola.

"Test?" I asked.

"Every presidential candidate," said Andy, "has to prove they have been tested in the real world under tough circumstances that they came through and that made them stronger. This will be your test!"

I looked at him, blinking, then turned my gaze to Viola.

"Victor was a crazed man," said Viola, adopting a conspiratorial tone. "He couldn't stand the idea of an America with a mythical creature roaming around in it. He attacked you. You had to defend yourself. You regret the loss of life, but do not apologize for doing what you had to do to survive. Everyone will understand that. And they will respect you for it."

I would like to report that their enthusiasm was infectious, but I cannot. The more they talked, the more I believed I had to get away from them. Nothing good was going to come from my association with Viola and Andy. Yet, as far as I could see, I was trapped with them. I had no option other than going along with them until I could find my way to freedom. Underrated as it was.

"Well," I said, "that sounds marvelous. I'm on board."

I couldn't tell if they believed me or not. They clasped their hands in front of their chests, then raised their fists in the air in a victory celebration, whooping as they danced around in circles, locking arms and moving their feet with wild abandon.

At that moment, maybe for only a few seconds or so, I decided they were possessed of a little bit of charm. Not an excessive amount, but enough that I smiled at them, despite my misgivings about their plan.

"Now," I said, "how about that suit?"

Andy broke from their dance and came over to me and tried to put his arm around my shoulder, but, of course, he was too short for that, and instead ended up by reaching high and patting my ribs.

"You got it, man," he said. "Come this way."

We went down the dark corridor together, him with a delighted spring in his step, me clop-clop-clopping on the tiled floor.

"We should get you some decent shoes, too," said Andy.

"That would be nice."

"Not those awful metal things, either. The kind that they pound nails into you to keep them in place."

"Right," I said. "Awful."

"We haven't actually given that much thought," he said. "Have you?"

"Shoes?" I asked. "No, not much. I figured nature—or whatever—make me for this world. Otherwise I wouldn't be here."

"Good," he said. "That's a good attitude. Maintain that during the campaign."

The campaign for president is what he was talking about. That was still something that I was trying to wrap my mind around. I wasn't sure I was succeeding.

"What is this place, anyway?" I asked.

"Once it was a mine. They took copper and other minerals out of here."

"It's much too nice to have been a mine," I said.

"Well, it hasn't been a mine for a long time. After it got mined out, some people in the area turned it into a bomb shelter. A really nice one. People could have lived here for over a year without ever going outside."

"Marvelous," I said dryly.

"Isn't it?" said Andy, completely missing my sarcasm.

We came to a common area which was roughly circular and from which other corridors went off into darkness, like spokes on a wheel.

The common area was mostly empty except for a couple of tables and a few chairs. It didn't look like a particularly inviting area, not at that moment.

"Where is everyone else?" I asked.

"Everyone else?"

"Yeah. This place is obviously built for a lot of people. Where are they?"

"There is no one else," said Andy. "Just me and Viola."

We kept going, down one of the other corridors until we arrived at a large room that was outfitted with a sewing machine in one corner and tall mirrors against another wall. The lighting was soft. The room had the pleasant feeling of a place that witnessed a lot of happy tasks being performed.

I stopped in the middle. I saw bolts of fabric, lots of them, tucked away in another corner of the room.

"You ever make an outfit for a centaur before?" I asked.

He shook his head. "But clothes make the man. Have you ever heard that?"

"It sounds familiar," I said.

"It should, because it's true. Can you even imagine a male winning the presidency if he didn't wear a nice suit?"

I could certainly imagine it, but I didn't tell him that. Why antagonize the person who was soon to have the ability to stab me with pins and needles?

"Now you just stand where you are," he said, "and I'll get a stool."

I did as he asked. The ceiling was quite low. I could put my arms up and touch the white tiles. Andy dragged over a step stool and put it next to me and climbed its three steps so he was level with me. He handed me a notebook and pen.

"Write down what I tell you," he said.

"Sure," I said.

He unrolled a tape measure and went to work. For the next half hour he laid that tape measure against my neck, my arms, my back, and around my chest. He looped it around my horse's body, measured each leg, and an incredible amount of secondary measurement, including my knee, the fluff of my mane, the length of my fetlocks, the slope of my coronet, and the placement of my tail. All the while he barked out numbers to go with the features and I dutifully wrote them down in the notebook.

By the time he was finished I must have had close to a hundred measurements in long columns. He was sweating by that time. He coughed. I didn't like the sound of that.

"You okay?" I asked.

He waved his hand at me. "All done. Now I don't need you for a while until the first fitting."

Viola showed up at the door, all smiles and radiating what I could only call glee.

"My turn," she said. "I'm going to teach you how to die."

TWENTY-EIGHT

I laughed, figuring that was a joke.

But it wasn't. How did I know? This is how:

"I'm not joking," she said. "Come on."

Neither Viola nor Andy had any humor in them that I could discern. They were always deadly serious. Literally.

"I've had plenty of near death experiences," I said.

"You shouldn't have any," she said. "If you want a successful life."

"What are you two yammering on about?" asked Andy. "Get out of my workroom, I have an outfit to design."

"He gets cranky when he's being creative," said Viola. "Come on."

She took my hand. I didn't care for the contact. Didn't much like physical contact with anyone, but allowed her to escort me out of the room and down the corridor to another room.

"The people who were keeping themselves safe from bombs weren't interested in austere surroundings," I said.

"They envisioned a city under the ground. I think there were provisions and room for about a hundred. Did you know that is what anthropologists consider the ideal number for functioning societies?"

I didn't know that. I also didn't know if it was true. Maybe it was just something Viola made up.

"Presumably then," I said, "our society is more or less non-functional."

"Well," she said, "you've had encounters with society. What do you think?"

"People could have been nicer," I said.

"There you are."

"Are we the only three down here now?" I asked.

"Yes," she said. "When we heard you were in the realm, we repaired to here and arranged to have you brought here."

She said it like it was the most normal thing in the world. Like an errand. Like they had gone to the store to get some ice cream to eat with the cake they had made earlier in the day. That kind of tone.

When I didn't say anything, she answered a question that I hadn't asked.

"For the purpose of making you the leader of the country," she said.

"Yeah," I said. "So I understand."

We came to another room, a large one, darkened. We entered and she turned on the lights. I saw it was the weapons cache. Numerous firearms lined one of the walls. They were polished and looked like they had not been used.

"Looks like they were a little worried about attacks," I said.

"Nothing wrong with being prepared," she said. "But that's not why I brought you here. You're a mythical creature. You should have a mythical weapon."

She went to an opposite wall, where I saw bows hanging from mounting hooks.

"No," I said.

She retrieved one of the bows and handed it to me. I didn't take it, not at first, but she stood there, holding it like it was a piece of gold I needed to have.

And here's where things got a little strange. Up to that moment I wasn't interested in a bow. Not at all. I didn't want to hold one or use one and I certainly did not ever want to learn how to use one.

But just seeing it in her hands, and noticing its construction, how it curved around to a graceful arch, how the string connected both ends with a tension that promised an execution of power, well. What can I say? I was seduced. It was made of some deeply rich and black material. It had shock absorbers attached to the curve, two of them, and it was big. At least six feet tall. Much too big for Viola, but not too big for me.

My hands wanted to pick it up.

Viola just held it in front of me, a small smile on her lips, barely visible, but unmistakable in its meaning.

"I know you want this," she said.

She was right. I reached out. She put it in my hands.

I knew exactly what to do. I held it by the handle in the center of the arch. I extended my hand to its full length, with the bow in my fist.

I reached out my other hand. Viola thoughtfully had an arrow ready for me. I took the arrow and notched it into the string, then pulled the string back.

There was unexpected power in the bow. My hand trembled a little, but I rallied and steadied myself so that all the tension was in the string. I pointed the arrow at a wall.

"It's okay," said Viola.

I held the arrow for a long time, reveling in the power it gave me. This was not like the firearm I had held earlier. That was some kind of anomaly, a weapon with no soul. It was only crude force, the gun. But this. This was an extension of me. This was my will flowing through a beautiful arch.

I released the string.

The arrow zipped through the air with a kind of preternatural sound, as though it was pulling up sound waves from some region unknown to mortals.

The arrow stuck in the wall and vibrated. It felt like it had not flown to the wall, but just appeared out of nowhere. It hummed briefly, then trembled and was still.

Viola handed me another arrow. I shot it at the wall.

Another.

I kept taking arrows from her and continued to stud the wall with them.

When I had shot about a dozen, she stopped giving me more arrows.

"Just as I thought," she said.

"What?"

"You're a natural. Andy thought you would have to be trained on the bow, but I didn't think so. I knew your ability was going to be built in. Instinct. You didn't like holding a gun, did you?"

"No," I said, "I didn't."

"There's a reason you're holding a bow in the constellation."

"That isn't me," I said.

"How do you know?"

"Because I'm here. Now. Talking to you."

"Someone could paint a picture of me and put it on a wall. Just because I'm not on the wall, doesn't mean the picture isn't me."

I shook my head. "Why does everyone talk in riddles?" I asked.

"That wasn't a riddle."

"You know what I mean. Strange talk. Talk removed from real life."

She turned around and went to a workbench. She grabbed something off the wall that I couldn't see, then turned around and ran at me.

She held a knife in her hand, raised above her head in attack mode, and she let loose a wild scream that went down my human spine, crossed the threshold to my horse hide, made my tail snap up in surprise, and froze me in place.

The scream did not die down as she advanced toward me with the pace of someone intent on committing harm.

TWENTY-NINE

Did I think she wasn't really going to hurt me?

Yes. I was sure she was, in fact. Why wouldn't she? She was crazy, just like Andy. They both were, living in the ground, grabbing me from the church, making me think I was something special.

I stepped back, startled, but had nowhere to go. My hindquarters hit a wall.

I raised my front legs high to try to scare her. My head hit the ceiling.

That was a mistake, obviously, because it didn't stop the attack.

She brought the knife down. It missed me, barely.

I am tested 

I felt an anger rise up in me that I thought had been erased by weariness. But it wasn't.

It started in my horse belly and moved up quickly to my human chest. My head felt hot and thick as Viola slipped and sprawled on the floor by my hooves. She laughed.

Which only made me more angry. I wanted to trample her. She didn't seem to care. Or maybe even notice that she might be in danger. She threw the knife to the floor so it skittered across the room and ended up hitting the opposite wall.

My rage subsided somewhat at that point. She scrambled out from under me.

"What was that about?" I asked.

"See what you're made of," she said.

She stood up and dusted herself off and stood in front of me, grinning.

"You wanted to know if I would hurt you," I said.

"Bingo."

"Quite a gamble."

She shrugged. Her nonchalance was even more enraging. I wanted to show her that I was not the complacent creature she seemed to think I was.

"How extensive is this facility?" I asked.

She blinked. "What do you mean?"

"I mean, how many rooms? How far does it go?"

"We told you. It was supposed to a self sufficient underground city."

158   I prepare to escape

"No such thing," I said. "Nothing is self sufficient. Everything depends on everything else. You can be cut off from the outside world and outside supplies for a time, but that's always temporary. Never permanent."

"You're the centaur philosopher now?"

"Just stating a fact. I don't believe you and Andy are the only ones running this operation."

She looked to the side. I didn't know exactly what that meant, but it seemed like it might mean she had not been telling me the truth, or that she was preparing to tell an untruth. In any case, I felt like I had stumbled on a vein of deception buried in their tale.

"Listen," she said. "We saved you from the guys who were going to kill you."

"Seems like you'd be just as happy to see me dead."

"We want you to be president," she said. "Not dead."

"Then why the weapons?"

"To protect yourself. To have a show of power. Voters like to see a candidate wield power. Real power. Ability with a bow is something anyone can see and feel."

While we spoke, I was edging toward the door. I don't think she noticed, not at first, but then some recognition flickered in her eyes and she stepped forward with her hands up.

"Don't run," she said.

"Try and stop me," I said.

"Don't do it!"

But I was long past listening to her. I stepped through

the door and saw the hall went down a long way. I began trotting down the hall. My hoofs made a terribly loud clattering sound on the floor. I dropped a few calling cards behind me, just to let Viola and Andy know what I thought of them. It felt absurdly pleasant to do that. It felt like I was giving them the middle finger and disgusting them all at the same time. A smile broke out on my face. I wanted them to see that.

I heard Andy's voice behind me. "What's going on?" he asked.

"The crazy bastard is running away from us," said Viola.

"We should go after him."

"No," said Viola. "He thinks he's figured something out. We should just let him do what he needs to do."

I thought that was an exceptionally wise thing to say, though I didn't tell either of them that.

The corridor's lighting dimmed until there wasn't any light at all. It was extremely difficult to see, but I felt air coming from in front of me, so I assumed the corridor went on for some time. I slowed my pace, but kept going. I felt the wall next to me as my horse flank rubbed against it.

I pressed back with my hands.

I slowed even more, and stopped.

In the darkness, my breathing filled the space and sounded a little ominous, as though I needed to scale things back, as though I was too big for the enclosure.

I stood for some time. If I kept going, I didn't know

160   I am disoriented

where I was going to end up. If I turned back, I would have only Viola and Andy waiting to greet me. Not a particularly welcoming thought.

I could also remain where I was. That was even less attractive. After all, I didn't know *where* that was, and I also didn't have any provisions. How long before I would starve to death?

I felt like I was in a dead zone, neither here nor there, with no way out and no way to know where or what I was.

I strained to look ahead. Only a grainy grey darkness. My eyes contrived to put motion in the scene, but I knew it was not perception. It was only wishful thinking. The workings of a brain trying to fill the space around me with—

—something. Nature abhors a vacuum, and so does a human brain.

Then I saw my phantom double.

He glowed in the darkness. Not so much that my eyes were dazzled or anything. Not so much that he could light the whole corridor, but enough that I could see ahead a little distance at least.

He walked in front of me. His horse head nodding. His big nostrils snorting the air. How I envied him that nose. I wanted to have nostrils that big. I wanted to take in great gobs of air to feed my horse lungs. Instead, I was constantly panting from the meager gulps I could obtain from the atmosphere around me.

I couldn't tell if my double knew I was following. He

gave no indication of awareness that I could tell. He merely stepped forward, using his own glowing, I imagined, to light the way.

We walked like this for a long time. At least a mile or two. The corridor went on for such a long time that it began to deteriorate in quality. First the polished floor gave way to bare ground. Then the ceiling and walls went from finished smooth surfaces to bumpy rock facades. Water dripped from the top of what I would now have to call a tunnel rather than a hall.

I heard bits of rock falling around me.

All the while I followed my phantom.

Until he disappeared. Completely. Just vanished into the rock. It was as though he slipped from this world to some other world, a world I did not have access to.

I stepped forward to the place he had entered the rock. I put my hand on the rock. It was cold and rough. Wet. I couldn't see anything.

I stepped back. My rear end hit the opposite wall, also cold and wet.

I was lost and could see no way forward, literally.

That was about the time that the ground started shaking, and big pieces of rock tore off the ceiling and began crashing down around me.

THIRTY

At first I didn't worry too much about it. After all, my own phantom had brought me here, he must have had a good reason.

But as the quacking worsened I began to see that my faith in my phantom was possibly completely misplaced. I strained to look ahead and see if he was there, but I did not see him or any evidence that he had been there.

I did hear Viola calling to me.

"Cal! Come back here. You're not safe there."

I didn't need her to tell me that. Rocks fell on my hindquarters. They didn't cause permanent injury, but it was clear that I was not going to survive much longer if the shaking continued.

I decided I might as well press on.

I stepped over an increasingly irregular ground, with rocks of every shape and size, from the smallest of pebbles to the irregular chunks of rock bigger than my phantom's horse head.

I slipped a few times. My hooves bit into sharp edges and my knees hurt, all four of them. I was beginning to think I was not going to survive this.

But then the shaking stopped.

I estimated it had gone on for perhaps fifteen seconds. An earthquake, so I assumed. What else could it be?

I had some knowledge of earthquakes. They shook for a time, then stopped. Did I need to know anything else about them? I searched my memory and my knowledge for more facts. I dredged up a vision of crumbling cities, buildings collapsing, people running in terror, horses rising up on hind legs from terror and galloping aimlessly in an attempt to find solid ground that wasn't there.

The image of destruction was accompanied by a feeling of melancholy. Not mine. It was put over the scene, as though a painter had dipped a brush into a pool of sadness and then dripped it over the crumbling buildings and loosening ground.

My own feeling at the time, completely divorced from the image that I had somehow conjured, was fear. I was in a dark place with no way to see forward. My hooves, as though of their own accord, did not want to take any more steps, since doing so might cause me injury.

I began to see that my hooves might hold more wisdom in their fibers than all of the contents of my skull.

So I stopped.

Water still dripped everywhere. I did not hear Viola any longer. Maybe she gave up. Or maybe the tunnel had become closed off.

I put out my arms to feel for the rocks. I touched the walls of the tunnel, then shuffled over and allowed my hands to follow the contours of the wall. I ended up running my hands over a jagged façade. I pushed, but there was no yielding. The rock was piled high and solidly in place.

I was trapped on one side.

I turned, carefully, and put my hands forward. I met no resistance, only air. So I stepped forward as carefully and slowly as I could, to keep from stepping on uneven ground, or putting my hooves where they might be damaged.

In this way I pressed forward and made slow painstaking progress. The darkness was so complete that my eyes began to conjure images for me to see. I caught glimpses of light, but knew they were imaginary. They did not illuminate anything before me, only offered some shimmering patterns that could not have corresponded to anything before me.

I called out for help, but no answer came.

Was I completely on my own? It appeared so. And if I continued on this path, where would it take me? I was so disoriented that I no longer knew which way was forward and which was back. I felt like I had been spun around against my will and was now set on an unknown path.

In this strange half place, I wanted some assurance that I would end up in a warm and inviting world.

But as I continued to make my way forward in the dark, completely blind, the ground began to shake again.

Aftershocks.

The word came to my mind unbidden from some depths I couldn't understand.

The shaking was at least as powerful as the initial quake.

I heard all kinds of terrible cracking and crumbling noises. That was the sound of the world coming to an end. I was sure of it.

The thought hardly ripped through my mind when a

particularly large rock tore off the ceiling and hit my shoulder. It made my knees go weak. I fell forward. I put out my hands, but found nothing to hold me. Another rock struck me on the side, tearing my fur open. I felt blood drip down to my belly.

Overcome by weakness, I fell over on my side. I tried to hold myself from hitting the floor of the tunnel with too much force by putting out my hands, instinctively, as though that could keep me from hurting myself.

More rocks fell around and upon me. I covered my head with my hands and scrunched forward.

It was a most undignified and sad way to die. I wasn't ready, but I saw there was little alternative.

I wasn't sure exactly what prayer was, but the concept rose up from the fathomless reaches of my brain's interior and I did whisper a very faint request to the cosmos:

Make my death swift and painless.

THIRTY-ONE

But I didn't die. Obviously, or I could not write this account.

As the rocks rained down on me, I rose up out of my body, a ghostly image of myself. I did not know I was going to do this until I actually did it.

I continued to rise, up through the rocks. They laced through me. I felt the veins of the earth rake my ghostly flesh. I swam up and up until I reached the surface and pushed myself onto the flat ground. There I floated for some time, reveling in the feel of the sun on and through me, the rays slanting an infinite number of trails through my field, which is what I was at that moment.

I felt a pull back to the earth. After all, my corporeal body was still there. It must be dead, I supposed. It must have been crushed under all that rock.

I recognized the terrain around me. It was the land which the armored vehicle had traversed before I had been trapped by Viola and Andy. I saw the tracks still there, heading in the direction of the cliff's edge. I followed the tracks to the edge again, and looked over.

And what should I see, but Viola and Andy making their way up the path from their underground shelter. I called to them, but they did not hear me. It seemed I had no ability to make sound in this realm. I was a ghost, after all, a kind of unleashed soul floating in the world.

But I was held close to my body. I attempted to run from the scene. I was able to do so for only a short distance, then my feet, grabbing at air, were unable to find true purchase. I ended up raking the air around me to no effect.

Why I tried to run is another question. I was horrified by the thought of seeing my dead form and didn't want to subject myself to that image.

Instead, I retreated, back to where I had emerged from the ground and I hovered over what had, by that time, become a scene of immense activity. Viola and Andy had converged on the area, but they had been joined by a small army of workers. They had drilling equipment and earth moving gear. There were also a lot of people. Easily five or six dozen. They held shovels and picks and milled about the area, ready to dig into the ground.

I watched as they began. The dirt they removed was piled up to the side, a great mound of it.

I tried to listen to the group, to hear some sound, but none came. It was an eerie, silent tableau before me. Sound waves brought nothing to my ears, but I was able to watch the scene.

I considered the possibility that I was watching nothing more than a dream. I tried to pinch myself, but could not. I didn't know what that meant, exactly. Sensations I had grown to understand and experience as my own suddenly seemed completely foreign. It was as though I was in a foreign country in which I knew none of the customs or ways of being.

As I hovered above the scene, my phantom double appeared on the other side, also watching.

I stared at it, and felt sorry for it.

I had acquired all the limbs, six of them. I reveled in my four powerful legs, and my two useful arms. The being before me, as vaporous as me, translucent and ghostly, had no arms. His horse's neck was planted firmly on top of his human belly.

He glanced at me. We locked gazes for a time. I tried to gather some feeling from him. Perhaps he was doing the same thing, I wasn't sure.

168 Communication woes

He approached me. I had an urge to run from him, but chose not to. He could not be dangerous, could he? I decided if he was, then I would accept the consequences.

I held my position until he sidled up right next to me.

He bobbed his horse head up and down, apparently wanting me to do something, but I couldn't tell what.

He snorted air. I heard it. Or thought I did.

"We can hear each other?" I asked.

He bobbed his head emphatically, indicating a yes.

"That's marvelous," I said.

A nod.

That seemed odd. Why didn't he say something?

"They call me Cal," I said.

A nod.

"You knew?"

Another nod.

"What's your name? Where did you come from? How long have you been a ghost?"

He tossed his head back and forth. I assumed that indicated the opposite of yes. Or, at least, that he didn't know the answers.

"You can't talk," I said.

Another nod.

Well, that was disappointing.

"Your corporeal being died?"

A nod.

"Blink with your eyes," I said. "How long ago? In years?"

He picked up my idea right away and blinked five times.

"You've been floating around like this for five years?"

A nod.

"Did your host body die?"

A nod.

"Was it around here?"

He shook his head. I wanted to try to figure out where the host had died, but didn't have the tools to dig out that information.

What I really wanted to know was what I was supposed to do next.

"I'm going to be lost," I said. "Aren't I?"

A non-committal trembling from my phantom double.

"I'm not looking forward to being a ghost."

He tilted his head. I took that to mean that my worries were unfounded. It would not be so bad.

"You're the anti-centaur," I said.

He nodded.

"We shouldn't even be here," I said.

Another nod.

"I'm tied to my body," I said. "I assume that means it's still alive?"

He tilted his head again. I decided that meant he didn't know.

We watched in silence as the diggers and the machines worked diligently all day and then night fell and they set up floodlights in the area and they kept digging, furiously, as though they were working against a deadline, which they were. My deadline.

I thought about going back into the ground, meeting up with my body again, and welding our realms back into one, but the thought of descending through the rock gave me pause. I did not want to do that. Not anymore. I liked the feeling of the open sky.

Dawn came. The sun burst over the horizon and flooded the area with natural light, lots of it. They turned off the artificial flood lights. Many diggers had descended into the pit they had built. They worked methodically and steadily. I admired their resolve.

Camera crews from what I assumed were television news operations arrived. The crew from *ESCAPE!* were there, too. I noticed that the news crews did not want them there, and there were a few altercations that involved pushing and shoving. One of the news crews even attempted to destroy some of the equipment of the *ESCAPE!* people. Police officers intervened and brought some order to the proceedings, such that the different crews were allowed their own space each and didn't infringe on the other.

Meanwhile, the work of digging kept going.

About mid-afternoon, with me and the anti-centaur still floating above the scene, I saw that the workers were excited. They called to each other, and they put down their picks and shovels and bent down and began tossing up rocks and dirt by hand. The hole was a good thirty feet or so. A chain of workers moved material up and out of the hole.

I floated to an area where I had a more direct view. What I saw sent a shiver of recognition and fear through my whole being.

I saw a bloodied patch of fur. My fur.

They had reached my body and I felt the stirrings of the horizon call to me. I felt the need to flee the area for my own sanity. If I kept watching, I thought my hearts would break into pieces.

THIRTY-TWO

But my hearts didn't break. Neither of them.

Instead, I watched as the remainder of my body was exposed to the air. The diggers slipped a large tarp under me, and a helicopter was brought in. It hovered over the pit and let down lines, which the workers attached to the corners of the tarp.

I felt a sense memory of having been hoisted like this before, and remembered my beginnings in this world, when I was found on the trail.

The helicopter brought my body up and then laid me gently down on the ground, some distance from the pit.

An army of medical folks, human doctors and veterinarians, descended on my still form. They inserted IVs, took measurements, and began artificial breathing for me. I had some difficulty seeing through the group as they labored over me. I knew I was down there, but I didn't think I was going to survive.

"Am I dead?" I asked the air.

I looked up, hoping to find some hope in the anti-centaur, but he was gone.

Heartless being, that one. How did he ever live? Or did he?

He might be even more of a mythical being than I was.

The team continued to do things to my body that seemed equal parts abusive and helpful. I didn't know what I wished for. Life, surely, was to be my destiny, because without life there was nothing. But what kind of life could I look forward to?

The team stepped back. They applied some kind of electronic gizmo to my chest and my horse's rib cage.

I jolted. I saw it.

And I felt it.

In my own ghostly form.

There was also a tug, as though someone had looped a rope around my waist and was pulling me down, like a balloon.

I resisted, but could put up nothing effective against the force.

Before long, I was accelerating down to my body and re-entered it with a jolt. Everything shook. I vibrated for several seconds, then became aware of hands and machinery manipulating my body.

It was disconcerting, to say the least. I tried to climb

back out. The violations were nothing I wanted to have continue. I wished only that I could be released. I opened my eyes. I was lying on the ground, dust and dirt all around me. Blood still pooling somewhere. Fluids were coursing through me, colder than they should be. I felt them crawl up my veins and arteries. I felt them like long claws of some monster.

My brain grew foggier. How could that be? When I was a disembodied spirit I had clearer faculties. Now I was a piece of meat on the ground that these people were finding ways to violate. They were inventive, I'll give them that.

I moved to rise to my hooves, but they had numbed me so I could not stand. I kicked, not knowing what I would connect with. They all stepped back. I heard shouts. "More sedative! Now!"

I didn't want any sedative.

"Don't touch me," I said.

"We're trying to save your life," someone in a white coat with a mask over her face said.

I was prepared to kick her, and everyone else. I had moved my legs around. I didn't know where they were, but I knew I could flail and if I connected, I would find something. Could assert myself in that small way, at least.

But the voice stopped me.

"Allison?" I asked.

She pulled down her mask and grinned at me.

"You remembered?"

How could I forget? She was one of the first people to help me. Really help me.

"What are you doing here?"

"I heard about you being buried alive."

"I wasn't," I said. "I was dead."

"Well, whatever happened, you're back now. We committed a miracle. Your leg healed up nicely. Now hold still while we save your life again."

Of course she was right. Allison was right. She knew what to do.

I relaxed completely.

That's when things got hairy.

"We're losing him," said someone above my head. "Heart rate down and erratic. He's going into arrest."

The words sounded ominous, but only for a moment. Then they sounded like sweet surrender. I looked up at the sky. It was so blue. A blanket that I wanted to pull over myself. Close my eyes forever and never have to deal with this world ever again.

THIRTY-THREE

I was in a fog for a while. I didn't rise up out of my body. I felt some kind of jolts, far off in the distance. It was as though an earth tremor was letting me know things were not what they should be.

I didn't care. Nothing mattered. This was no doubt from the sedatives they had administered.

I knew I had a pain in my chest. I didn't know how severe it was, and it didn't matter because even though I knew about the pain, I didn't feel it as pain. It was just something in my field of experience that I noted and tucked away in the back of my brain.

Then I lost consciousness.

When I returned to the living, I was no longer on the ground. I was standing in a relatively well-appointed living room. There was a high ceiling, and high windows to match. I had a view of a city. Which city, I could not tell, but there were tall buildings and they went on for some distance. Obviously a lot of people lived here.

There were others in the room with me. Five of them. They wore thin white coats of the kind Allison had worn.

I was standing.

There was a couch in front of me. A large one. One that looked like it was big enough for my bulk.

"Where am I?" I asked.

"You're safe," said one of the people in white.

"That's an opinion," I said, surprised by my own words. "Give me a fact. Where am I?"

"In a building in downtown Portland, Oregon," she said.

"How did I get here?"

"It's complicated," she said.

"Another opinion. I'm tired of them. Where's Allison?"

"She'll be in soon. She wants you to be comfortable."

"I have to piss," I said. "And shit."

"There's a bathroom built to accommodate you down the hall," she said. She pointed to a corridor.

I stepped toward it. The carpet under my feet felt strange. The cushiony spring of it was not the way my hooves wanted to interact with the world. They wanted dirt. The earth of the world.

I stepped down the hall, feeling like a fool floating on clouds. I was too high up. This wasn't right. I wasn't meant to live in a high rise.

The bathroom door was tall and wide. I stepped inside. An over large toilet was in one corner. Obviously a custom-made fixture. Surely no manufacturer made such a large toilet on a regular basis. A huge shower stall was installed in another corner with correspondingly large brushes and wash cloths. The bathroom was large enough for me to move around easily and comfortably.

I did what I had to do, the plops of my waste on the water so amusing that I had to laugh out loud.

I had a very satisfying draining of my bladder. It felt like I was releasing all the tension in the world.

When I emerged from the bathroom everyone was gone.

I blinked.

I was alone?

It appeared so.

The kitchen table was laid out with a large spread. I found chicken, salad, plates of beans, chips and salsa, vegetables and several varieties of dips, and a bowl of fried rice. The portions were generous. Whoever saw to all this was cognizant of my needs. I ignored the view out the windows and settled down to a feast.

As I ate, I saw a remote control on the other side of the table. I grabbed it, looked around for a screen, found it on the living room wall, and pressed the power button.

Imagine my shock and surprise when I saw myself on the screen. I almost stopped chewing. Almost. I was famished and nothing was going to keep me from eating.

Still.

There was film of me on the ground where they dug me out. I was being called the miracle centaur. People were moved by my plight. They donated money. Lots of it. Enough for the foundation—*the foundation!*—that had been set up in my honor and for my benefit, to buy a loft at the top of a building in Portland Oregon and convert it into my apartment.

Then I was moved into it.

All this played on the screen as I watched. It was a surreal moment, perhaps even more surreal than my first fall on the trail, which now seemed like ancient history.

The report on my new circumstances finished. I had lost my appetite completely. Half the food remained on the table.

I switched off the television and felt the room around me. It was as though the world had turned inside out. I was no longer the outsider. I had an apartment, a relatively plush one. It was designed for me. Made comfortable and convenient for my needs. I should have been pleased. Even overjoyed.

Instead I was deeply suspicious. My experience was that humans did nothing out of altruism. They always wanted something in return.

And I had nothing to give any of them.

THIRTY-FOUR

Someone burst through the door to the apartment.

I turned around. Allison came striding in, followed by Viola and Andy.

"Well," I said, "a welcoming committee?"

"Of sorts," said Allison. "How is everything?"

"Remarkably comfortable," I said. "I'm grateful to everyone who made this happen. I think."

"You think?"

"I miss the ground."

Allison nodded. "I understand," she said.

Viola and Andy trailed a large suitcase on wheels.

"What's in there?" I asked, pointing at the suitcase.

"Your clothes," said Andy. He bent down and unzipped the top and pulled out a large folded garment. There was a lot of material. He was weighed down under it and staggered to place it on the couch near me.

I didn't move toward it.

"Go ahead," said Viola. "Andy worked on it for some time. We want to see how it fits."

I suddenly did not want to have these people watch me while I put on the garment.

They all noticed that I wasn't moving.

Allison clapped her hands together. "Right," she said. "We should give you some privacy. Don't take too long. We have a lot of stuff to go over."

"What stuff?" I asked, instantly wary.

"Don't worry about it right now," she said. "We'll be back in five."

I looked at the folded thing on the couch. It appeared to be quite complicated. "Better make it ten," I said.

"Ten it is," said Allison as she ushered the other two out the door and closed it behind all of them.

I picked up the garment. It was heavy. I unfolded it on the couch. I could see that a lot of excellent workmanship had gone into it. The material was soft and comfortable. It had a crispness to it, but did not seem like it would irritate my skin. There was a shirt tucked into it as well, and a tie. I searched my memory for the steps necessary to tie a tie, and found it was there, as I should have expected.

I took the shirt by the collar and shook it in the air. I put it on and buttoned the buttons. An alien feeling, to have a piece of cloth on my chest. But not an unpleasant one. I found the protection it afforded me quite attractive. Was this why people wore clothes? Because it felt safer than without them?

The tie could wait. I tossed it aside.

Now the outer garment. I wasn't sure what to call it? A

jacket? Maybe. But it was larger than a jacket. I unfolded it and saw that it was the length of my body.

It was going to be awkward putting it on. I wrestled with the part of it that trailed off and was, I suppose, intended to cover my horse end.

I put my arms through the sleeves. They felt even more protective. It was as though someone had come down and put armor on me. The sleeves ended at my wrists. My hands felt like they were disembodied for a moment. It was strange to look at my arms and see this fine material covering them.

The rest of the garment was draped to my side. I twisted my torso around and scooped up the length of the material and tossed it back, then shook my hindquarters to allow it to drape down.

I saw that Andy had some decisions to make when he constructed the thing. Should he try to make pant legs for my horse's limbs? He had obviously decided not to. Just as well. I don't know how I would have gotten my legs into them.

Instead, he opted for a kind of revised blanket effect. The material he used was thinner, a nod to my own fur that didn't need a lot of heavy material, obviously.

It wasn't just a blanket attached to the jacket, either. It had a feel of something made to order. It fell smartly down both sides, with a short length all around that gave a kind of dignified curtain effect.

I trotted into the bathroom where a large mirror adorned one wall.

I stood in front of the mirror. I did convey a regal aspect, as though I was imbued with earthly power, a lot of it.

I stood to the side and saw that the rest of the garment, the part on my horse aspect, added to the effect. I was no longer half horse, but wholly a being with my own integrity. I was a centaur of splendor.

I trotted out of the bathroom with a new sense of my own self. And then I faltered. Was I now a completely domesticated thing? Had I lost all my wildness?

And what if I had? It had not done me any good. I was a wild thing when I arrived and my trials continued. Everyone wanted to tame me or kill me. But now? People wanted to feed and dress me. Like a pet, perhaps. Or maybe like a revered being?

I mulled over the possibilities, none of which felt like they fit me very comfortably, certainly not as comfortably as the clothing I was now wearing.

I heard a tap on the front door.

"Come in," I said as I pulled at the lapels of my garment, straightening them to look as smart as I possibly could.

Allison, Viola, and Andy came tumbling in, beside themselves with admiration.

"Oh," said Viola, "that is lovely. You look handsome."

"Looking very smart," said Allison. She beamed.

I challenge Allison

Andy had a look of concern on his face. "How's the fit?" he asked. "It looks pretty good. I was concerned about the back, where the human part joins the horse part. That was a little tricky, but it looks fine."

"It looks more than fine," I said. "Can I have more of them?"

Andy laughed. "So you like it?"

I shrugged. "Of course. Who wouldn't?"

"That's great," said Allison. "Now Andy and Viola have to go."

"Go?" I asked.

"They have a court appearance."

I looked at their faces. They looked back at me with what I can only describe as mortified dread.

"They kidnapped you," said Allison.

"We have to face the charges," said Andy.

Viola handed me a bow, which I had not seen before. "You keep practicing on this," she said.

I took the bow. It felt strange to be holding such a weapon while wearing a suit of clothes.

"Go, go," said Allison, practically pushing them out.

They said their goodbyes and were gone.

Then it was just me and Allison.

"I never thought I would be doing this," she said.

"Doing what?"

"Caring for a centaur."

"Are you caring for me, or are you keeping me as a pet?"

She didn't answer. I don't think, in her place, I would have had an answer either. The question came out of its own accord. I had not planned the words.

"I saved your life," she said.

"And now you want a reward?"

"Look," she said, "the press conference is going to be in only two hours. We have to prep you."

"Press conference?"

"Yes, of course. It's where you are going to announce your run for the presidency."

THIRTY-FIVE

I suppose it is odd to say that her statement was strange in my ears. After all, everything about my life on planet Earth to that moment had been strange. My very existence was deeply strange. And Viola and Andy had already told me about my candidacy for president.

"No," I said. "I don't think so."

"No?" she asked, directing her question more to the air than to me. "No? You don't say no to this. Your current digs are courtesy of a lot of people who want something in return."

There it was. The hidden benefits of altruism.

"That's not my choice," I said.

"No mythical creature has ever run for president before. Do you know that while you were comatose, there were calls to have you classified as an animal? I fought that. To protect you."

"Thanks," I said.

"You're welcome. Thanks to me, you are classified as a human being."

"And that's a good thing."

"Yes."

"Viola and Andy said they wanted me to be president. They were crazy. Just like you are."

"Listen to me," said Allison. "This is a good thing. You will gain recognition. You will be the people's choice. Everyone loves you. They think you are their savior."

"I don't know why they would think that."

"Have you looked down at the street?"

I shook my head.

"Go," she said. "Go look now."

I sighed and stepped toward one of the tall windows and angled my view to the sidewalk and street far below. I did see many people milling about the building. They had, it seemed, even blocked off the street from traffic. No vehicle could have traversed the street.

"So," I said. "Some people want to disrupt traffic."

"They are all there for you. You."

"Doesn't mean they'll vote for me."

"You are a fool," she said.

"Not my fault. We are what we are."

"If you don't run," she said, "if you don't announce at the press conference, you'll lose all of this." She extended her arms, taking in the space of my apartment. My apartment. The place I had already grown to love in the short time I had been here.

I hesitated, not knowing what to say to her at that moment.

"There," she said. "You see. You want this. It's all yours if you do one small thing."

"Deciding to try to run the country is no small thing," I said.

"You'll have me to help you."

That was another thing. Why was Allison suddenly so interested in a political career for me? She was a veterinarian. I studied her face, trying to see something in her expression, or her eyes. She wasn't exactly a blank, but she also didn't relinquish much in the way of information.

"You're a long way from your roots here," I said.

"It was time for a change."

"Tired of fixing animals?" I asked.

"This is bigger than veterinary work. This is a chance to change history."

"That may be important to you, but it isn't to me."

She pulled out her cell phone and tapped it and held it up to her ear. I heard the distant muffled ring.

"Yeah," she said after someone picked up. "He's resisting."

Some silence as she listened.

I felt myself getting nervous, as though the floor was going to open up under me.

"Yeah, we can do all that. Looks like he won't change his mind, though. I was afraid of this."

More silence. She wasn't faking the phone call. I heard a voice on the other end.

Some people came in the front door. They were a camera crew, carrying a video camera and sound equipment and lights.

Allison noticed them and held up her hand. They froze. They also looked at me with what I can only describe as a mixture of awe and fear.

I was torn between two instincts: either to step forward and deepen their fear, or step back to give them some comfort and feeling of safety. Instead, I remained where I was, on the border between the two. The tension in the room increased. It was as though no one truly knew what to do in this situation.

"I can have him out of the apartment by the end of the day," she said. "Actually, probably in the next hour."

Bewildered looks from the camera crew.

Allison tapped the connection closed, then looked up at me. "You sure about this?" she asked.

Was I sure? I didn't know. I still held the bow that Viola had given me. She had also left a few arrows. They lay on the table next to the uneaten food.

I picked one up and held the bow in my hand and notched the arrow against the string and pulled the string back. The arrow was aimed at the floor. Then I raised my arm, taking the bow with it and directed the aim of the arrow directly at Allison.

THIRTY-SIX

The string was trembling in my hand. Allison looked directly at me. The camera crew was cowering, which made me smile inside.

"What are you doing?" asked Allison.

"I'm not sure how long I can hold this bow like this. I'm tired. I'm shaking."

I wanted her to say that then I should drop the arrow down and ease off the string, but she didn't say that. "You have a decision to make," she said.

"What decision?"

"What are you going to do with that bow?"

Again I glanced at the camera crew. They seemed so bright and vivid in my vision, as though they had stepped out of some preternatural painting.

Their initial fright seemed to have dissipated, because they decided to record what was going to happen next. One of them motioned to the others. Another raised her camera and put it on her shoulder and aimed it first at me, then panned over and held the lens on Allison, who *still* did not flinch or move.

My frustration with the world, I think, led me to this standoff. I had been shot at so many times that I felt my only recourse was to shoot back. It was Allison's bad fortune to be the one in the way of my frustration. It wasn't my fault. Or, at least, in that moment, I had convinced myself that it was outside forces that led me to the place where threatening someone who had helped me was the proper course of action for me to take.

"We can do this all day," said Allison.

I imagined the arrow leaving my bow. The hushed silence from the camera crew was more unnerving than what might have ensued if they had been loud and taunting me. I didn't want that silence to continue.

"What do you think?" I asked them. "What would make a good video?"

No answer. This irritated me even more.

They swung the camera from me to Allison back to me and back to Allison again.

"Don't know where the focus should be?" I asked. "The killer or the victim? Bet you wish you had brought two. A split screen recording of the event. That would be worth quite a bit, wouldn't it?"

Still no answer, although their reticence to speech was perhaps an answer in itself. They did not need to say anything, since I held the stage, as it were. I was orchestrating this event.

I moved the bow to the side, so the arrow was no longer pointed at Allison, but rather at one of the tall windows behind her. I released the arrow. The arm holding the bow instantly relaxed and the bow fell from my hand.

The arrow struck the window and shattered it into a

shower of crystalline pieces. They cascaded to the floor then lay still like wounded animals. Allison still did not move.

The camera crew surged forward, training their lens on me as I held up my hand in front of my face.

A strong wind came in through the space where the glass had been. It swirled around the apartment. It was not a deafening wind, nor was it the sort of wind that would cause any kind of damage.

We all stood in the swirl of it, me reveling in the feel of nature in this artificial space. The others—well, I didn't know what they felt. They didn't tell me.

"That make you feel better?" asked Allison.

"Don't know yet," I said.

"I do," she said. "It made you feel worse."

"No," I said. "I don't think that's true."

"Destruction is not the way to enlightenment," she said.

The camera crew trained their lens on Allison. She didn't seem to appreciate the attention. She indicated that they should frame my face, and so they did. They got close. I imagined the resulting image was going to be me, filling any screen that would display their video. Everyone eventually watching would see only my face, not the rest of me. Not the part of me that made me something other than human.

"You should photograph my rear end," I said. "Give people something to laugh about. 'Here's the horse's ass.'"

"That's no way to begin a campaign," said Allison.

"There is no campaign," I said.

She retrieved her phone and tapped it.

"On the contrary," she said, and held it up to me.

I saw my face, reddish and startled, backgrounded by the very room I was in. They were live-casting this. Anyone with any interest at all had witnessed what I had just done.

"No," I said.

Allison nodded. "Yes," she said. "See the numbers at the bottom?"

I looked again. A crawl of numbers, yellow on a red background, moved from right to left.

"Those are your polling numbers. They are high. Very high. They spiked when you held your bow on me."

"So the electorate is blood thirsty?"

"They appreciate someone who takes matters into his own hands. Who isn't afraid to shake up the situation."

"And that's what I did?"

She nodded. "Now I think it's best for you to go stand by the open window."

I trotted to the pile of broken glass in front of the empty space where the window pane had been.

The arrow, I guessed, must have gone through the space and into the void, since I didn't see it. Who knows where it landed? And the glass that didn't fall into the apartment? It must have fallen to the street below.

"Do you feel the love of the people?" asked Allison. "Do you feel how they want you? You are a mythical figure.

I make a decision  191

The country doesn't get many of those. Not even once in a dozen generations. But here you are."

The camera, meanwhile, looked like it was floating above the floor. It was as though the operator behind it was a ghost, unseen and unheard. I saw only the lens, trained on me.

Instead of being shot at, I was being shot. Nothing felt better. Nothing felt like it would ever be better than this. The entire world was watching.

Allison stared at me, encouraging me to say something. This was my time.

The next five seconds were the quietest and most profound five seconds of my life. A decision was in the offing. I had only to make it. The people wanted me, if what I saw on Allison's phone could be trusted. The lens of the video camera came closer, closer, always closer, as though it could never get close enough. As though it wanted to come within chomping distance of my mouth, where it would be chewed up and swallowed by me.

My thoughts were aswirl with trepidation and a sense of urgency, both at the same time. I wanted only to be accepted. Was this acceptance?

"My name is Cal," I said. "And I want to be your leader."

I held the space for another second or two, keeping the silence. Letting it fill the spaces of the world, wherever those might me.

Then I turned around, displaying my hind end to the

camera, and stepped forward, smartly, toward the welcoming void.

THIRTY-SEVEN

I heard Allison's objections, that was the first thing.

"No, Cal. Don't. Don't do that."

It was a welcome sound, her cries for me to reverse course, but it didn't stop me. I had these visions of me stepping into the air. I would fly, for a few seconds, then hit the street below, a tragic figure, lost to the world, but there as a symbol—of something. A fallen leader? I wasn't sure what.

Best to leave while I was still on top, wasn't that the way to go out? Wasn't that the way to assure my immortality?

I had only a few steps. My hooves knew what to do. They stepped smartly. I was aware of wanting to present a stately and regal demeanor. I wanted to make sure everyone knew I was not some sad case. No. I was a strong-willed creature, capable of the most dramatic of gestures executed with aplomb and the stature of a strong character.

I was fully prepared to continue. I was that far from achieving my destiny, which was to take control of my own life, even if that meant ending it, when I felt multiple hands on my clothing.

They gripped the portion of the garment that covered my horse's aspect, which wrenched my human aspect back so that I felt pain at the place where horse and human met.

Crunching glass  193

Was my back broken? I didn't think so, but I wasn't sure.

I leaned forward. The wind blew through my hair and over my ears. It whistled. The sound was welcoming. I wanted to be in that realm.

"I'm immortal," I said to those holding me back. "Don't you know that? I'm a mythical being. I live for the ages, not for this one age."

Was anyone still recording this? The hands holding me back, and they were numerous, had to belong to the video crew. Where was Allison? After her initial call for me to halt, I did not hear her. Or see her. But I had focused my vision and my will on the void in front of me. I was less than a foot from the lip of the void, where the floor met the sky. Glass crunched under my hooves and the feet of those holding me back.

We strained like this for some time. How long is impossible to say.

I kicked behind me. I connected. Not sure with who, but I felt the pressure of a body on my hoof and I heard the sound of someone falling away.

The others shouted. Incoherent sounds. Like panic. But the pressure on my garment did not abate. Instead, it felt like I was being held even harder, against my will, completely against anything I could possibly want from the world, these strangers were keeping me from the sky.

Finally, after much too long a time, after the stately import of the moment had been completely and irrevocably ruined, and I was just some animal that had to be corralled, Allison spoke up.

"Let him go," she said.

They didn't. Not at first. Our tug of war still gripped us both.

"Release him," said Allison. I twisted my human part around. Allison was well behind me, standing with her eyes ablaze, like she *wanted* me to die. Could it be?

"He's not worth it," she said, while staring directly at me, her words meant for me as much as for the five or six people who had gripped my garment and were holding me back.

And, I can only guess, her words were also for the audience, the people watching this drama unfold.

My would-be rescuers clung to me like a colony of parasites. Did they not understand the nature of freedom? Did they not see that they were imposing their will on another? Did this not bother them?

"Listen to her," I said. "She knows what she's talking about. I'm not meant to live here. I should die."

"That's good," said Allison. "I like your spirit."

I turned from her. I was tired of her. She saved me once, and she was trying to save me again, but there was no point to it. I knew that. Everyone must have known that. Everyone watching.

Except at that moment I suddenly realized no one was watching. Not then. There was no one recording the proceedings. Not anymore. The camera lay to the side, its lens trained on the feet of the couch.

I was breathing so hard that my lungs felt like they were going to burst. The strain of pulling against my would-be saviors was getting to be too much for me. I was faltering. My weakness in the face of the oppressors was a shameful thing at that moment. I wanted to obliterate that shame in the only permanent way I could imagine.

"You're not Pegasus," said Allison. "You know that, right? You won't fly. You'll die."

"I know that," I said, and then, even while I was straining with my horse legs to go forward, I began unbuttoning my garment. They could only hold onto the cloth. If I slipped it off, then they could no longer restrain me.

The buttons were difficult to slip through their button holes, as the fabric was pressed so hard against my chest. So instead of unbuttoning, I gripped each button, one by one, and popped them off. There were seven of them, and each one took some doing to remove, but in my state at that time, I must have had super human strength. I was able to methodically tear off each button.

Once the buttons were gone, arcing into the air through the open window, I was being held only by my sleeves.

All I had to do was let my arms go back. The garment would slip off and they would have no hold on me and I would go forward.

 ## I endure great pain

I dug in with my hooves. I reached for the void, my arms extended forward as far as they would go.

And then I relaxed my arm muscles and let my arms snap back.

THIRTY-EIGHT

In that instant, the feeling of freedom overwhelmed me. Here was what I was looking for, I thought, from the moment I arrived I needed this release. The world had tried to give it to me, with the numerous shots taken at me, the many threats on my life. It was a message I should have heeded. The world knew I didn't belong. It was just waiting for me to see it, too.

And I did see it. Finally, there in an apartment on the top floor of a skyscraper in Portland, the vision of what I was or should be coalesced into a meaningful picture of my destiny. I yearned to be a broken being on the concrete below.

But before the garment slipped off completely, before I had my complete freedom, I felt a sharp stab of pain in my rear, just below the hem of my garment.

It weakened my knees so I stopped surging forward. My garment slipped off my arms and I heard the falls of several people tumbling to the floor.

I twisted around.

I felt wobbly. Dizzy and not right, as though the world had suddenly been plunged into water. I dropped to my knees. A man in a white coat stood next to me. He had a hypodermic needle in his hand, apparently the thing that had stabbed me.

And he stood and grinned at me. I glanced at Allison. She wasn't grinning, but she seemed happy with this turn of events. Had she orchestrated it? Probably.

The last thing I remembered was the camera crew getting to their feet and gathering their equipment and training their lens on me.

Again.

And then I was in my bedroom. Curtains drawn across the tall windows. A kind of murky darkness enveloping me with something that was not quite comfort, but not quite despair. It felt like a twilight place, the sort of existence I had grown accustomed to, indeed, the sort of existence that defined me: trapped between two worlds. Made of two entities with an uneasy border between them.

I had a pillow behind my head. The pillow rested on my back and my human portion was bent way way back so that I was using my own horse portion as my bed.

My legs were locked in place, the knees like bolts that held me in place. I did not know how long I had been asleep. I raised my human portion and unlocked my knees. I tossed the pillow into a corner and trotted to the door.

I opened it and stepped out into my apartment.

I was met with an army of people. They sat behind computer terminals and were grouped in tables, several of them. The living room of my apartment was a control center of some kind. Everyone was so serious. They all glanced up at me, then stopped whatever they were doing.

"Good morning," I said.

On the other side of all these people I saw the window that I had broken was covered with a large piece of plywood. A strange symbol of my aborted attempt at suicide.

"I *said*," I said, "good morning."

They threw some weak "good mornings" back at me.

Allison, who had been in the back, stepped forward. "The campaign is going well," she said.

The campaign?

"I have to go take a leak," I said.

I turned from them and trotted down the hall to the bathroom. I did what was necessary, feeling the relief of letting waste go. Then I emerged from the bathroom and went into the kitchen.

"I'm hungry," I said.

"Did you hear me?" asked Allison?

"I did," I said. The people behind their computer terminals went back to their tapping and typing. They didn't appear to have any interest in me.

"How long was I asleep?"

"Quite some time," said Allison.

"Do you think it's okay to drug a candidate for president?"

"We had to save you."

"Who was that with the needle?"

"A friend."

"Yours or mine?"

"Both."

"Oh, I doubt that," I said. "A friend, a true friend, would have let me go over the edge."

"You can't believe that."

I shrugged, unsure if I did or not.

"You have some appearances today."

"Appearances?"

"The public wants to see you?"

"What public?"

"You don't know this, not yet, but you are polling monster numbers. The Democratic and Republican candidates have nothing on you. You are the most viable third party candidate this country has ever seen. If you hold your position for the next two weeks, you will be elected president."

"An office I have no qualifications for."

"The constitution says the only qualification is that you be over thirty-five and that you are a natural born citizen and that the electoral college elects you. You are clearly over thirty-five, just from your appearance."

"There's no birth certificate for me that I know of."

"Don't worry about that. Medical evidence will suffice. If we have to, we can produce DNA that shows your age."

"Good for you," I said.

"And we found you, fallen from the sky, on a trail within the legal boundaries of the country. So you're a natural born citizen."

"That wasn't exactly a birth."

"Close enough," she said.

"And no one has challenged this? No one from the two big parties?"

"They are afraid to. Any time they say anything against you, your poll numbers go up."

"Did I not already ask for food?" I said. "I'm hungry. I need to eat something. I need to eat a lot of something."

Allison looked disgusted. "That's all you think about?"

"Most of the time, that's all I *can* think about. I have a horse's body to nourish through a human mouth."

"We can fix that," said Allison. "Intravenous feeding. It will relieve that aspect of your daily life."

"Yum," I said. "Fluid from a bag. Now who wouldn't want that for their breakfast?"

She stared at me. I stared back, then turned from her and went to the fridge and opened it and found a lot of carrots. A ton of carrots.

I laughed. "This somebody's idea of a joke?"

"We couldn't find hay," said Allison. "We've got someone on it."

"I don't like hay."

"We determined it was the best food for you."

I shut the fridge door.

"Allison," I said, "where did you ever get the idea that I would be a good president?"

Before she could answer, a campaign worker came to

her and they bent their heads together and whispered some words between them.

"Hey," I said, "I'm the candidate, however reluctantly, so no secrets from me, hmmm? What's going on?"

Allison straightened up and looked at me. Her expression was shock, mixed with puzzlement.

"Well," I said. "Out with it."

She cleared her throat. "Seems they found another centaur."

THIRTY-NINE

"Are you going to run this one for Secretary of the United Nations?" I asked.

"I'm serious," said Allison.

"So am I," I said.

The news of another being like myself might have been interesting to me. It would have been natural for it to engender some kind of response. Hadn't I been looking for my tribe? Didn't another centaur have to be part of that?

But the bare fact of another centaur did nothing to rouse my interest, which was interesting in itself.

"You don't seem to care," said Allison.

"Why should I?"

Allison shooed away the person who had given her the news.

"We've been looking for another centaur," she said.

"Good for you."

"You need a running mate."

"And only another mythical being could possibly qualify?"

"Exactly."

"Allison," I said, "what's in it for you? Why are you so interested in me being president?"

She ignored me. "The new centaur is close to here. They found her on the same trail where you appeared."

"Must be some kind of portal there," I said. "Flotsam from another world comes through and ends up here."

"You're not flotsam and neither is she, but I think I see what's going on."

"Really?"

"You were unique. Now you're not."

"What will that do to my numbers?" I asked.

She turned away from me, apparently in disgust. Which was fine with me. I wasn't much interested in talking to her anyway.

I pulled some carrots out of the fridge and began methodically eating them. I went through at least twenty carrots before the taste and texture of them began to make me gag.

I did find some cheese and bread in there as well. I sliced some of the cheese, put it on the bread, and ate half of the loaf before *it* began to repulse me. I was still hungry.

"How about pizza?" I said to the room. "Is it too much trouble to order a dozen pizzas and have them brought here? Does anyone care about the well being of the candidate?"

Someone in the back of the room stood up.

"I'll order some pizzas," she said.

"Make then all large," I said. "And mix them up. Some vegetarian, some meaty, some exotic toppings. Surprise me." I grinned. She grinned back. Reluctantly, but still it was genuine when it finally filled her face.

"The new centaur told us her name," said Allison. She had a phone pressed against her ear.

"Good for her," I said.

"She calls herself Sprig."

"Sprig," I said, barely holding back a smirk. "What kind of name is that for—well, anything?"

"She's young," said Allison. "A kid, actually. No more than eight or nine. She has no memories from before. Just like you. Her memories start at her appearance on the trail."

That got my attention. How did a child end up here? "Where is she?" I asked. "Is anyone taking care of her?"

Allison's face registered disappointment. Such a young centaur could not, obviously, be my running mate.

"They have her at a military base in Eastern Oregon."

"We need to get her out of there," I said.

"We don't have that authority."

"I don't care," I said. "Let's go there."

Everything in my being changed when I learned her age. She must be scared. Frightened to death. She was surrounded by beings who were not like her. She needed someone she could recognize.

"Cal," she said, "be reasonable. I've already told you you have appearances today. You have a campaign to attend to. You cannot go gallivanting off on some side trip to appease your vanity."

"Vanity?"

"You want to help someone who looks like you," she said. "That's vanity."

Oh, Allison had a way about her. She was always so sure of herself. She always knew exactly what was right and what was wrong. Or so she thought. I wasn't at all sure she knew anything about anything. Certainly not about me.

"Where am I supposed to be?" I asked.

"There's a ribbon cutting for a new solar energy plant being built in Arizona. We think you should be there. We have a special plane ready for you."

"Okay," I said.

"We also have an appearance planned at the wall."

"What wall?"

"You remember, the one between Texas and New Mexico. Texas is trying to succeed from the union. They put up a wall around their state."

"And we don't want them to succeed?"

"No," she said. "We want to keep the union together. If Texas goes, then other states will go, and the whole enterprise will collapse. We think you standing at the wall and demanding that it be torn down will help hold the union together. After all, you are a combination of disparate parts. You know what it is to live in harmony with discordant aspects."

See, what was I just saying? Allison was always so sure of herself.

"I'll do both of these appearances," I said, "but only if we then go to see Sprig."

Her mouth twisted into a crooked line, as though she was trying to corkscrew her face into her mouth. It made me laugh.

"What?" she said.

"You are trying to contort this into something you can use to your advantage," I said. "But this isn't about your advantage. It's about what I want."

Allison *looked* like she was thinking it over, but I think she was more or less pretending to think it over.

"Okay," she said. "You do the appearances, then we go see Sprig."

"When do we leave?" I asked.

She looked at her phone. "In an hour."

"Excellent," I said. "Then I have time to eat my pizzas."

She shook her head, completely disappointed in me, obviously. She thought I would rise to the challenge of trying to become president. She knew nothing about centaurs.

Not that *I* did. I just happened to be one.

"I'm giving you a lot of leeway," said Allison. "Considering your origin. And what you've had to endure."

"Very generous of you," I said.

"But we need you to be all in. The country and the *world* needs you to be all in."

At that moment my ghostly double emerged from the wall on the other side of the apartment. It floated above the workers, all of them still tapping on their computers. It hung, suspended in the air just below the ceiling. Its horse head nodded and its human legs kicked behind it, like it was trying to swim through the air. It made me think of a bizarre frog, armless, with a strange head.

Then he saw me. We locked gazes. He zipped right up to me, so he was inches from my face and then he leaned close to my ear.

I think I *felt* his words rather than heard them. No one else saw him. Or, at least, no one else reacted to him.

"She's your daughter," he said to me.

FORTY

I had no reason to believe him. He was, as far as I knew, a figment of my imagination, and as such, might be only some kind of projection of my own wishes or dreams or— well, who knew? Errant thoughts. Bogus beliefs.

After he said what he had to say, he receded from me and went back into the wall.

"You okay?" asked Allison.

"Not sure," I said.

The pizzas arrived. A large stack of white boxes. The

smell of them filled the apartment. My mouth started watering. My hoofs clopped in the direction of the food.

"Okay," said Allison. "You're hungry. I get it. You're always hungry."

"My curse," I said. "One of them. I've got a lot of curses hanging over me."

"If I had a violin, I'd play it," she said.

But I didn't care about that. I took the first box, opened the lid and dug in. I polished off the pizza in about two minutes, scarfing it down with gusto. I felt it go into my cavernous stomach, way down below me.

People stopped what they were doing and watched me. I didn't care. I opened the next box. Still hot and aromatic. The cheese was still bubbly. The toppings were still sizzly. I ate that one and asked for water. Someone brought me a bottle. I chugged it.

Allison had a disgusted look on her face, which I barely noticed as I tore open the next box and continued eating.

I was aware, on some level, that my eating was more than just for sustenance. I had the excuse of my horse part that needed a lot of nourishment, but my eating behavior at that point was not about sustenance. It was about stuffing myself so I wouldn't feel anything. I didn't want the other centaur to be my daughter.

"Cal," said Allison.

"What?" I asked between mouthfuls.

"The plane leaves in half an hour."

"You want me to get dressed?"

"That would be nice."

"I'm thinking about that suit I had."

"Yes?"

"It's not really me."

"If you're going to run for national office, you have to wear a suit and a tie," she said. "You *have* to."

"I'm the outsider. I should dress like one."

She sighed. "What do you want to wear, Cal? A saddle?"

"I'd like to go with nothing. I have fur on most of me. The rest of me can be bare. Bare-chested. Isn't that synonymous with strength?"

"You can't go bare-chested. It's not acceptable. On any level."

"A T-shirt, then. A nice one. In a gem color."

"We can arrange that," she said.

"Good. I'll go jump in the shower. Just as soon as I finish this pie."

I ate another twenty or twenty-five slices, opening boxes as I went. Then downed another bottle of water.

After that I went to my specially built bathroom and quickly took a shower. They had thoughtfully arranged to have blowers installed, big ones that dried off my fur in nothing flat. A nice touch.

I stepped out and Allison had a T-shirt ready for me. It was salmon-colored. I put it on and immediately felt like I was somehow more ready than I had been.

The T-shirt ate my personality.

I have no other way to describe it. As soon as I put it on, I wanted to do the appearances that I had previously dreaded. And I no longer wanted to go see the new centaur. The one that might be my daughter.

"Let's go," I said.

We left the apartment. Allison came with me. We were both surrounded by armed guards. Four of them, dressed in black, as though they were clothed in pieces of the night. None of them introduced themselves.

"Who are these guys?" I asked Allison.

"Don't get to know them," she said. "If they end up dying while protecting you, you will have a broken heart. Two of them."

I felt my own hearts beating at that moment. The redundancy inherent in the dual existence of blood pumping machinery did not give me any comfort.

"How did you arrange all this infrastructure around me in such a short time?" I asked.

"Not that short," she said. "You were out for two weeks."

"Still."

"I set up a kickstarter. In less than 24 hours we got a couple of million dollars. That was enough to remodel the apartment and get a staff in place."

I shook my head.

"A kickstarter campaign?"

"Why not? It's very efficient. Obviously."

"Obviously."

We took a flight of stairs at the end of the hall. They had thoughtfully arranged to have a flight specially built for me. It was wide and the steps were extra large. Large enough for me to stand on all fours on each of them.

When we finally emerged onto the roof, the fresh air of the great outdoors hit me with a bracing sense of energy. I wanted to run. Gallop, even.

But of course there was no place to do that here.

A helicopter awaited us across the roof. It was large and its blades were already turning.

"Let's go," said Allison. She hit my side with her flat hand. I didn't like that. I was not some horse she could order around. I deliberately slowed my pace as we approached the helicopter.

"What's wrong with you?" asked Allison. "We have an appointment to make."

"Don't be hitting me," I said.

We had to talk loudly over the noise of the helicopter's blades and engine. The air pushed at us, trying to knock us down. We had all stopped while I did my best to convey to Allison that I was not to be struck as I had been.

"You don't slap human beings like that," I said.

"You're not a human being."

"I'm not a horse, either," I said. "So don't treat me like one."

She rolled her eyes and put up her hands. "Fine," she said. "You want your dignity. Is that it?"

I didn't answer her. Instead I turned and approached the helicopter.

The four men in black followed me. This must have been some kind of specially built helicopter. It was huge. I was able to walk in standing up. There was no seat there for me, but there was a comfortable area with enough room for me to stretch out. I stood and waited.

The men in black got in after me and then Allison. The pilot turned and waved at me. I waved back.

Then Allison shut the door and we were off. We rose up and kept going until we were a good forty feet above the roof, then we angled to the east.

"We're going to get a flight at the airport," said Allison.

"With a specially designed plane for me?" I asked.

"Of course."

"I don't care about that other centaur anymore," I said.

She blinked. Several times. "You sure?" she asked.

"She's not my concern," I said.

"Everything's your concern," she said. "You're running for president."

"You know what I mean. I can't expend energy on her situation."

"You sure about this?" asked Allison.

Whatever feelings of empathy or sympathy I had were gone. I cared only about myself at that moment. I cared only for the campaign.

"You could all die in the next instant," I said to Allison,

indicating everyone in the helicopter with a sweep of my hand, "and it wouldn't bother me one iota."

"That's good," said Allison.

"Do you really think so?" I asked.

Here she stopped and waited for some inspiration to come to her. She wanted to agree with me. She wanted to be a team player and take part in the brutality of a campaign. She wanted to seem as powerful and right.

But she couldn't. I could tell.

"No," she said.

"No?"

"I've cancelled the two appearances. We're going directly to the centaur."

I could have rescinded the cancellations. I could have directed all my minions to see to it that I was at the solar station and the wall.

But I didn't.

And I was glad I didn't.

FORTY-ONE

We landed at the airport. I got out of the helicopter and my inclination was to run. In fact, I stepped away from the group with determination and a sense of freedom rising. The four men in black moved closer, as though to try to hold me in place, but I knew they couldn't do that. If they tried, I could trample them. And I would have.

They must have sensed it. Allison too, because she motioned for them to leave me alone.

That gave me the opening I needed. The tarmac was spread out before me. Beyond it was a river. There was a low fence between me and the river, but I knew I could easily jump over that. I had the power and the will.

I took several steps toward the fence. I imagined running along the bank of the river. I wanted to feel the wind through my hair and over my fur. I yearned for the ground to push up against my hooves as I pounded back on it.

It would all have been so easy. Leave everything behind. Find a place, perhaps an island, in the river. Swim to it. Live there on my own. It seemed like the ideal life at that moment.

But I didn't do any of that. Didn't gallop across the tarmac. Didn't jump the fence. And certainly I did not find an island to live on.

Instead, I asked Allison where our plane was.

She pointed to a spot some distance away where I saw a small craft awaiting us.

It, just like the helicopter, had been configured to allow room for me. I boarded and stood, my thoughts of running free on hold for the moment.

Everyone strapped in and we got underway. Once we were airborne, I saw that the airport was situated next to a wide river that went on for miles in both directions, eventually lost at the horizons.

"When you're elected," said Allison, "this will be Air Force One."

"It's very nice," I said.

"We do our best," said Allison.

I looked out a window at the passing landscape below us. "What river is that?" I asked Allison.

"The Columbia."

"It's beautiful."

"Yes it is," said Allison. "It starts in Canada and meanders for twelve hundred miles, then widens considerably before emptying into the Pacific Ocean. Natives used to take enormous runs of salmon from this river."

As I watched the river through a window, I also saw that several craft were chasing us. Some drones and two other small planes.

"Who are they?" I asked Allison.

"Paparazzi," said Allison. "People are very interested in you. They want to know where you're going."

I made a face in the window and put my thumbs in my ears and waved my fingers at my pursuers.

"Don't do that," said Allison.

"Why not?" I asked. Then stuck my tongue out.

"Stop that!"

I leaned back so my face was no longer in the window. "Don't you ever want to have fun?" I asked.

"You don't want to let people see you doing things like that," she said. "It's bad for the campaign."

"You know who I miss?" I asked.

"Who?"

"The *ESCAPE!* people. They made my life interesting. You, on the other hand, make my life boring."

Allison looked down at her phone.

"There," she said. "See? You're already all over the place with your tongue hanging out."

She showed me her phone. I did look ridiculous, but wasn't that the point? The very fact that I was running for president and *that I was the leading candidate* was ridiculous.

"I don't think you understand the power of being a clown," I said.

"Clowns have no power. Where did you get the idea that clowns have power?"

"They get attention. That's power."

"Attention is not—" she stopped. "Oh never mind," she said. "We're going to land at the base soon."

"Already?"

"Short trip. You can use the few minutes we have to select a running mate."

"I don't need a running mate."

"Of course you do."

"No. I've been reading up on some of this stuff."

"Some of this stuff?"

"The constitution," I said. I had done no such thing, of course, but Allison didn't know that. At least I didn't think she knew.

"The constitution," she said, with a withering look. But I didn't wither.

"Yup," I said. "I am not required to name a running mate. And I don't think I will. I stand alone. *That's* power."

Allison's mouth hung open. She was not ready for that response from me. I didn't even know if what I was saying was true. Maybe I did have to name a running mate, maybe I didn't. But I did get her attention, that's for sure.

She narrowed her eyes and looked at me with what I hoped was respect, but who knows? It might have been contempt. Or something else.

"We'll put out a press release to that effect," she said.

"Excellent. Now I think I'll take a nap. Presidents do well when they nap. I should get in the practice."

I leaned back, locked my knees, and closed my eyes.

That's when the plane lurched. Everyone fell down, including me.

Then the plane leaned way over to the right before straightening out into a steep dive.

FORTY-TWO

We all slid to the front of the cabin.

"What happened?" I shouted.

Allison shook her head. "Don't know," she said. "Something's very wrong."

The four men in black did not say a word. They pulled out guns from their jackets and crawled toward the cockpit as quickly as they could. I watched as one of them shot the cockpit door, directly at the handle. It splintered and the shots were deafening. Then they kicked the door down and received gunfire from the cockpit.

"Stay down," said Allison.

I was not the least bit inclined to challenge her. I kept myself pressed against the floor.

One of the men in black took a shot and fell away from the door. The other three kept shooting into the cockpit. Whoever was behind the controls took a few hits, I was sure. I couldn't see the pilot, but I saw blood on the floor and the walls, and a hand slumped to the side, still gripping a weapon, which then slipped out and clattered to the floor.

"We're still diving," I said.

Two of the men in black grabbed the pilot, who I assumed was now dead, and lifted him out of the seat and dragged him out and into the main cabin, and threw him onto their fallen colleague. All this was just a few feet from where I was sprawled.

Then the remaining man in black crawled down into the cockpit and slipped into the pilot's seat and grabbed the controls.

The plane leveled into a normal flight configuration.

"What the hell," I said.

"Someone just tried to kill us all," said Allison. "Congratulations. Your first assassination attempt. And you're not even in office yet."

218   Photographed bodies

She seemed unreasonably excited as she got up on her feet and went over to the two people who had been shot.

The two men in black that had hauled out the pilot came to me. "Are you alright, sir?" asked one of them.

"I'm fine. But your buddy."

"Hazards of the job, sir. Our only concern is your safety."

"You get pilot training?" I asked, indicating the one in the cockpit.

"Of course," he said, as though I asked him if the sun was scheduled to rise tomorrow.

"He's dead," said Allison. "Both of them."

Her tone was unreadable. I couldn't tell if she was excited or upset. Was this all part of the thrill of the campaign for her?

She photographed the bodies, crumpled on the floor.

"There," she said. "That'll go out on all the feeds. Let's get a picture of you," she said to me.

"No," I said.

"Come on," she said. "Stand over them. You've vanquished your would-be killers. The world should know."

"I didn't vanquish anyone. It was these guys." I indicated the men in black.

"They have to remain anonymous," she said.

"Is that true?" I asked them.

They nodded.

I sighed. "Allison," I said, "this isn't right. What about the dignity of death?"

She laughed. "Nothing dignified about a political campaign."

I looked at the pilot's body. He was still bleeding. The sight was more than a little upsetting. And the man in black. He had one bullet hole in him. It was not bleeding as much, but it looked just awful, like a hole into hell. They four of them had taken matters into their own hands. The men in black knew, most likely, that at least one of them was going to be hurt or killed, but reasoned that their superior numbers were going to prevail. On that point they were correct.

"The feeds already have the picture up," said Allison as she flicked her finger over her phone's screen. "Headlines are pouring in from all over the world. You're going to have to give a statement when we land. Now come over here. A picture with the dead pilot will ensure a landslide. You'll take all 50 states. I guarantee it."

I looked at the two men in black, looking for some kind of guidance here. I didn't find any. They simply returned my gaze with no expression of any kind. They would die for me, one of them *had* died for me, but they would not interact with me.

We began our descent. The plane was going smoothly and, so it seemed to me, entirely too normally. There had been two deaths on board this craft. That should have counted for something. Things should have been stranger than they were. The flight path of the plane should have been affected in some way.

But it wasn't.

I moved to a spot next to the fallen pilot.

"Who do you suppose he was?" I asked.

"Someone who wanted to die with glory," said Allison. "Killing a president or even an aspiring president ensures your name will have a place in history."

I wasn't sure that was true at all. It felt like something else must have been going on. Ideology must have had some hand in the attempt on our lives. Didn't it?

Allison held up her phone, pointing it toward me. "Don't smile," she said. "We want you to look fierce."

"Fierce," I said.

"Yup."

I bared my teeth. Allison laughed. "Not quite that fierce," she said.

"I feel like I should be holding a weapon," I said.

"Good idea," said Allison. "Guys?" She looked at the two men in black.

"We can't surrender our weapons," said one of them.

"Take the bullets out," said Allison. "It's for the camera."

They glanced at one another, as though they were actually considering the proposition, but then they shook their heads. "No can do," they said.

Allison displayed facial expressions that clearly indicated irritation.

"Come on," she said, but only half-heartedly. Even she

must have realized her request was never going to be granted.

"I could show a fist," I said.

She turned to me. "A fist is not enough," she said. "We need a weapon to shore up your win. Only a prominently displayed firearm will convey what we need to convey."

"And what is that?" I asked.

"We need to let the world think you're a baddass."

That made me laugh.

Which made Allison smile. Even the men in black got a chuckle out of it.

While they were thus engaged, I reached over and as quickly as I could, I reached into one of their pockets and grabbed his gun.

I held it above my head, pointing it at the ceiling.

Allison's smile went even wider. She snapped several picture in quick succession.

The men in black didn't know what to do. The other one, the one who still had his weapon, took it out and pointed it at me.

That's when I began to feel like my life was actually in danger.

And I panicked. I dropped my arm and leveled the weapon in my hand at the man in black.

FORTY-THREE

Allison kept taking pictures.

 I am abandoned

Both men in black were frozen. Neither moved for a second or two, then the one who had his gun aimed at me dropped his weapon and held up his hands.

Meanwhile, we had gotten closer to the ground. The landing gear was down and I saw buildings flash by us through the window.

"I'm sorry," I said, and dropped my weapon as well. "I don't know what came over me."

"The need to assert your power," said Allison. "That's good."

I put my face in my hands and shook my head.

I felt that everyone else in my vicinity was embarrassed for me. Allison stopped taking pictures.

"You can't transmit any image where he's pointing a weapon at us," said one of the men in black.

"I won't," said Allison. "I've posted one where he's holding the gun high above his head. See?"

She put her phone in front of the faces of the men in black while the plane kissed the tarmac with a slight bump, then slowed way down as it taxied in to its parking spot.

They seemed to approve of the image on Allison's phone, then looked at me. "Sir," said one of the men in black, "we can't protect you anymore. We are resigning."

"Wait," said Allison. "What? You can't quit."

"We will stay on until you find some replacements, but we feel we do not have trust from the subject."

They both bent down and retrieved their weapons and returned them to their side holsters.

"A little friction and you turn tail and run?" asked Allison.

They ignored her attempt to rile them up. "This is a crime scene," said one of them. "The police will have to investigate. We'll all have to give statements."

"None of that matters," said Allison. "Those are just formalities. What matters is that you continue to protect this—man."

"I'm not a man," I said.

The man in black who had landed the plane emerged from the cockpit, took a quick scan of the situation and said, "Looks like we're resigning?"

The other two nodded.

"I think maybe I won't," he said. "I like this guy. I want to help him."

"There you are," said Allison.

"I radioed ahead that law enforcement needed to board the plane immediately," he said.

"Thank you for being my protector," I said.

"I only want to be part of your victory," he said. "Some small part is all I require. I admire you, sir."

It sounded strange, that sentence. I wasn't sure it was sincere. On the other hand, I had no reason to think he was lying.

There was silence in the cabin. I felt like it was my turn to say something important or significant.

Instead I put out my hand. He took it and we shook hands. It was a moment I'll never forget. His grip was strong. It taught me to make my grip strong as well. I needed to convey an air of strength at all times. Wasn't that what a president needed to do? I was pretty sure it was.

"The picture of you holding the gun above your head," said Allison. "It's trending off the scale. Wildly popular. Over a million positives already. Told you it would be big."

We heard wheels rolling over the tarmac, then a bump at the side. The portable stairs had been pushed to the door of the plane. It opened. Cops with guns drawn entered the cabin.

"All secure," said the man in black who had piloted the plane. "Two dead. One suspect. One secret service."

I paid attention to how he was handling the situation. I noted an extreme lack of emotion, even though a terrible thing had happened not 15 minutes previously, and it included the death of a colleague of his, which meant it could easily have been himself lying dead on the floor. But he remained calm and completely in control of himself. I thought that was beyond admirable. It was fantastic. Incredible. I told myself that I should adopt the same sort of attitude to life and all that life was going to throw at me, if I did become president. After all, it would be my responsibility to send people into danger. All presidents had to do such things. It wasn't in the job description, but it was what they did.

The next few minutes was taken up with the police collecting our statements. I told them exactly what I saw and what I remembered. They took it all down. Allison and the men in black did the same. Our accounts more or less matched each other, which I assumed was good. The cops seemed satisfied with what we said.

Then we left them to their duties and walked off the plane and down the steps onto the tarmac.

I was immediately surrounded by people. Lots of people. They clustered around me and followed me as I made my way to a low building a quarter mile or so away. We were being led by a very formal looking man, dressed in a uniform, and walking with a determined pace, as though he wanted to get somewhere fast. I easily kept up with him, being part horse, but the others had to hurry to match his pace.

I saw more people coming in from all sides. Some of them carried signs. They were of the type that proclaimed their love for me.

The three surviving men in black made sure they were close to me, surrounding me as best they could. They were alert and ready to die for me. I appreciated that.

"What does it mean," I asked Allison, "that there are all these people?"

"They love you," said Allison.

I doubted that. I was something new and they probably liked the novelty of me. But love? Hard to believe.

"Just accept it," said Allison.

"I think I do," I said.

"Then act like it."

"What do you mean?"

"Wave to them."

As I trotted along, I raised my hand and waved. The crowd, still swelling in number and coming from all directions, answered with cheers and waves right back at me.

I felt an intense—something. It wasn't love, not exactly, but it was a feeling for these people. They had invaded a military base, apparently with no bad consequences, just to greet me and let me know they approved of me. That was a vote of confidence I would never have thought possible only a few days before.

We arrived at the building entrance, which was barricaded against the crowd and which had several armed and uniformed soldiers around it to keep it safe.

We went inside. It was suddenly quiet. I didn't like the quiet. I wanted to remain in the embrace of the raucous crowd. Wanted to feel their good wishes.

The man who had led us across the tarmac spoke.

"The centaur is this way," he said, and took up his quick pace again, while I tried to bring myself back to the moment. I had forgotten that we were here for a reason. I was to meet what my double told me was my daughter.

I wasn't at all sure that my double was correct, but I knew I had to meet her. Had to see her. She was the only being remotely like me in the world, as far as anyone knew. I should be there for her, if not for me.

We stopped at a heavy metal door, the kind with a small rectangular window in it. I couldn't see through it, however, because the man who was leading us was standing in front of it.

"She's mostly used to us," he said. "At first she was very shy, but after a while, once she got to know us, she became more willing to interact with us. She eats a lot. We told her about you, and that you were coming, but I'm not at all sure she understood."

I nodded. Allison said nothing. Uncharacteristically reserved. Was she trying to give me my space?

"We'll let you go in on your own. She likes flowers." He handed me a bunch of daisies, tied together around the stem with a rubber band.

I took them. "Thanks," I said.

Then he stepped back. I turned the door knob, bent my head low, and stepped through.

FORTY-FOUR

She was in a corner, eating. From what I could see, it was the remains of a pizza. She looked up at me. I froze in the doorway, halfway into the room. Someone pushed me from behind. I couldn't tell who. Allison? The guy who led me here? I didn't look back, just clip-clopped into the room.

I wanted to say something to her, but I realized no one had told me her name. Or even if she had one.

I took a couple of more tentative steps forward, then held out the daisies.

She seemed to sniff the air, as though trying to see if the daisies had a scent.

She made no move to approach me.

"Hi," I said. "I'm Cal. Did they tell you about me?"

She shook her head. She looked to me to resemble an approximately eight-year-old girl. Except for the horse part behind her. They had given her a pink sweater to wear, and had fashioned some kind of crude pink blanket that was draped over her back. Her little hoofs were covered in pink booties of some kind. There was a pink clip in her hair.

"You like pink?" I asked.

She nodded.

The thing is, she looked like a cartoon. Not that I would tell her that. It wouldn't have been polite. I had to keep from laughing. I think she saw my struggle. She looked down at the floor.

"Hey," I said. "I like pink, too."

It wasn't true. She knew it wasn't true. I knew it wasn't true. And she knew I knew.

"Um," I said, "what's your name?"

She looked up. "Star."

"A fine name," I said.

"I guess."

"You don't like it?"

She wasn't much of a talker, that was for sure. More given to long silences and stares down at the floor.

"They gave it to me."

"Hey," I said, "they gave me my name too. Cal."

She made a face like she had tasted something sour.

"Ha," I said. "Yeah. Terrible name."

"Are you really going to be president?" she asked.

"Don't think so," I said. "But some people around me think I will."

"Do you want to play hide and seek with me?"

"Maybe later," I said. "Right now, I'm wondering where you came from."

"I fell out of the sky," she said, but not very convincingly.

"Really?"

She shrugged.

"Do you remember that?"

She shook her head.

"So it's something they told you?"

She shook her head again. "You ask a lot of questions," she said.

She was right, and it wasn't getting us anywhere. "Okay, Star," I said. "I do ask a lot of questions. Maybe too many. I'll just ask one more. Do you know who your parents are?"

Star stared at me for a long time. Too long. I was beginning to think she had no more words. She had just run out. She stared up at me with wide eyes. Child eyes. They were—

—empty.

A sensation of extreme discomfort tickled the back of my neck and the hairs on my human back stood up and a shiver went down my human spine and crossed over to my equine spine where it ended at my tail, which jolted and flicked at the air.

"Star," I said. "Are you really here?"

That's when she flickered in the air. She dissolved into pixillated pink squares, hanging before me. Then she repeated a sentence several times, starting again and again as though someone kept hitting a reset button in the world.

"I uh—I uh—I uh—"

I turned around. "What is this?" I asked.

Allison came into the room. "Sorry," she said. Others trailed behind her. One of them walked through Star like she was nothing but colored fog hanging in the air.

"She's a hologram," said Allison. "And she's malfunctioning."

"I can see that," I said. "But why? What's going on?"

"We wanted to show you being empathetic with a young person. People like that. Enough footage of that gets out on the networks and you'll have more than a win. You'll have a landslide. I guarantee it."

I scratched my head, genuinely confused as to what all this meant.

"I could have been at the border," I said.

"This is more important."

The guy who walked through Star went to a corner of the room where a cabinet rested and opened the door and reached inside. A piece of electronic equipment was in the cabinet. He fiddled with it and Star was reduced to a vertical pink line, which then contracted into a pink dot in the air, which then evaporated.

"Or how about the solar farm? That was more important that this, wasn't it?"

"You still don't understand that everything is about image," she said. "Image image image. Get that through your head."

"I could have done this," I said. "I could have had a moment with a hologram. I could have sold it. All you had to do was tell me. Don't keep things from me."

"I did get some of the footage out," she said. "See?"

She held up her phone. I looked at the screen. I saw myself standing with Star, me talking about names. Her looking at me like I was daft.

"Surely that isn't anything good for me?" I said.

"2.8 million hits. In the first 90 seconds."

I wondered what my phantom could have been referring to when he said Star was my daughter? Obviously it didn't mean anything. I certainly wasn't a hologram. We could not be related. I had suspected that the phantom was just my own thoughts manifested in some ghostly image created by my own mind. Now, it appears, I had some proof. And I also saw that it had let me astray. Nothing good came of this faux meeting. I was almost killed just getting here.

"Are we done now?" I asked. "Can we go now?"

"In a minute," said Allison. She looked up at the others in the room. They looked back at her. There were the three men in black. There was the hologram operator. And there were two military personnel. They all had firearms. Some of them were visible in holsters, some were hidden. I saw them as bulges under their jackets. The combined fire-power in my immediate vicinity made me think that I had an arsenal always following me around. I was like the epi-center of a bomb. Or an assassination machine. I was death personified. I was the place where destruction happened. Not because of who I was, but because of who clung to me.

"Give us the room," she said to everyone except me.

There was some hesitation, then they all left us alone and walked out into the hall.

Allison and I stared at one another, neither of us, I guess, knowing what to say.

I spoke first. "I expect you sent everyone out so you could apologize to me in private."

She snorted.

I smiled.

"I just want to know one thing," she said. "Are you seri-ous about the campaign?"

I didn't have to think about it for even half a second. "No," I said. "Absolutely not. I never wanted to run for president. And you shouldn't want me to, either. I know *nothing* about this world. Nothing."

"I'm offering you the chance for power. Real power. All you have to do is help me. A little. Be charming. Be present. Be engaged. That can't be so hard, now can it?"

She had moxie, I'll give her that. She was not about to

let me stand in her way, even if it was me she was trying to mold into something.

"You haven't given me a good reason to want this," I said.

"You want a reason," she said, "I'll give you a reason. If you don't gain power, a lot of it, you'll be killed."

"What? No."

"Haven't you noticed how many times you've been attacked since you got here?"

She had a point.

"Let's make a deal," I said.

"I'm listening."

"You run a hologram in my place. I get to leave all this behind, and you get to be proven right about image being everything."

She backed away from me, as though I had told her I was on fire.

"Cal," she said, "I have given this campaign my all. I just want you to be on board."

"But that's just it," I said. "I'm *not* on board. You should realize that. You should allow me to be who I am."

"Who you are is a giant target. How long do you think you'd survive without protection?"

"So that's why I'm to be president? Because that would keep me safe."

"Safer."

"If I'm not wrong, a lot of presidents have been shot. Even more shot *at*. And several have been killed."

I watched as she thought about what I just said.

"I can drop all this right now," she said. "I can walk away from it."

"Put your phone up," I said. "Set it on live broadcast."

She did as I asked.

"Is it broadcasting everywhere?"

She didn't say anything, just breathed like she was angry. I'm sure she was.

She nodded.

"This is Cal," I said to the phone. "I'm a centaur. A mythical being. Maybe that's why you have given me a mythical stature, maybe that's why you think I can be your leader."

I paused for dramatic effect. Allison, still holding the phone, was clearly angry. Her lips were pursed and her face was red. She tapped her foot.

I pressed on.

"I appreciate all the support I've had," I said, "but I can never be your leader. I don't know enough about you or your country. Accordingly, I am quitting my run. I am no longer running for president. If you were going to vote for me, I urge you to give your vote to another worthy candidate."

Allison mouthed some words to me. I think she asked, silently, if I was finished.

I took a deep breath. "So that's it," I said. "I wish you all well."

Allison touched the phone's screen.

"We'll see how that plays," she said.

"It was the best thing to do," I said.

"You could have been something," she said. "The most powerful mythical being ever."

"I didn't want that," I said.

"That's because you're a fool."

She looked at her phone. "Two and a half million sad faces. In about 20 seconds." She shook her head. "Good bye, Cal."

Then she walked out of the room. She left the door open. I looked around, completely alone. What had I done?

FORTY-FIVE

A lot of my surroundings then disappeared. The room became transparent. I looked through the walls and saw the buildings of the base begin to evaporate as well. The walls turned into stacks of blurry blocks, then fragmented, and tumbled. Everything was gone except for the plane that had brought me, but the men in black boarded that, along with Allison, and some of the other officials, and it trundled down the runway, picked up speed, and was airborne.

I didn't want to run for president. The whole notion was absurd. But now that I had stepped away, I missed the rough and tumble of the campaign.

I looked around. I was in a field of grass: brownish, and dry. The sky was clear. A few white clouds on the horizon.

No wind. Just the cool air of the sky, swirling around me in a maelstrom of feeling, as though I was being wrapped in feathers.

I decided I was going to retreat to the wilderness. There were mountains in the distance. Probably meant there weren't too many people there. I could retreat to the peaks and find a life for myself in nature.

I could fashion a bow and hunt for my food. I'd live in a cave. Maybe people would come to me for advice and wisdom. I was sure I could find some of that in the wilderness. Nature had its own way of understanding things. If I could tap into that understanding, everything would be better for me.

I took a couple of steps forward, when I heard a voice from behind.

"Halt."

I turned around. A row of police officers were strung out in a line in the distance in front of me. They each leveled a weapon at me.

"You're under arrest," said the one in the middle. A large man. He held a megaphone, which is why I could hear him clearly even though he was a long way away.

"What for?"

"Trespassing."

"I'm leaving. Just let me go, and I won't be trespassing anymore."

"Doesn't work that way, sir. Stay where you are. We are going to apprehend you."

They walked forward, weapons still drawn and aimed at me.

I took a few steps back.

"Don't do that, sir," said the cop with the megaphone. "It won't go well for you."

I had a fleeting thought that they wouldn't shoot me if I ran, but there was no reason to believe that. And it would only take one to render me more or less dead.

I was reasonably sure I didn't want that. But then I started thinking about it. Was there anything in this world that I really needed or wanted? Was there any reason for me to be here?

I could go up on the mountain, but what was the point? Probably no one would come looking to me for wisdom. After all, I couldn't even find a way to live in polite society. I would always be the outcast.

The cops began running, the whole row of them, a dozen at least. Running toward me. They had a mission. It involved me. They were intent on catching me.

I didn't care. I turned my rear end to them, deposited a few road apples for them and began running for all I was worth.

A few rounds hit the dirt around me, sending up piles of dust, and delivering piercing stabs of pain to my ears. It only made me run faster.

Soon the shots stopped. I thought maybe they didn't have the heart to shoot me down. Or maybe I was too far away from them.

 I am wounded

I kept pounding the ground, my hoofs hitting the surface like I was asking the buried souls in the earth to come up out of the interior of the planet and present themselves to me and save *my* soul.

I hit the ground hard, again and again.

In front of me, the mountains, capped with an unbearable gleaming white, beckoned. I was going to go right up to them, and then I was going to climb them as far as I could, above the treelike, past the snow-line, to the peak. From there I was going to gaze back at the world. I was going to feel the cold air flowing over me, and I was going to be the happiest creature in existence, because I was free.

I was thus engaged, imagining my future, when an intense pain ripped through my shoulder. Before I could register the fact that I had been shot completely through, another round hit my side, tearing a streak through my fur and leaving a line of dripping blood.

I could have kept galloping, I suppose, but my heart was no longer in the run.

It wasn't so much the pain of it as the thought that no one in this world wanted me. It was a not particularly pleasant feeling.

I slowed my gallop to a trot.

I heard more shots behind me. Rounds whistled past me. Another shot connected with my body, this time on my rear end.

That's when I stumbled and fell to my knees.

I reached forward, as though I was going to break my

fall with my hands, but instead I bent back, back, back, so my human spine touched my equine spine.

I rested like that, for some time, until the officers of the law ran up to me and slapped handcuffs on my wrists.

FORTY-SIX

They weren't exactly gentle with me, and that was the part that bothered me the most. I was willing to accept the fact that I had to pay a debt to society, even if this society was not willing to accept me as a fully functional member.

But there was no reason to tranquilize with darts, which is what they did. There was also, in my estimation, no call for tearing away my clothing. But they needed to do that, to make me into more of a wild thing than a human being. Tipping the balance toward what made them more comfortable.

They took me to a wildlife park and put me in with some horses. They told me I would wait there until my trial. Some of the horses were retired from racing. Others were old and their previous owners didn't want them anymore. A couple of them were horses that police officers used to ride around on to patrol neighborhoods.

They congregated in herds, small ones and large ones. They ate grass.

None of the horses wanted anything to do with me. As soon as I arrived, they scattered, keeping their distance the whole time. I suppose I was too strange for them.

Keepers came and talked to me, though they didn't find me particularly interesting. I think I frightened them. They brought me food. Bland stuff. A lot of oats. I told them I couldn't just eat oats all day. They brought me bread. No imagination.

The park was in a remote location in Eastern Washington. They thought to keep me there, I suppose, to protect me from the meddling public, or so they told me. I wasn't sure if I should believe them.

The prosecutor found many things to charge me with. Trespassing, vandalism, firing a weapon recklessly, indecent exposure, vagrancy, and destruction of property.

I was assigned counsel. Her name was Mayel Johnson. She came to see me at the wildlife park. They gave us access to a barn where I could consult with her. They did not take away the handcuffs. I told Mayel that this treatment was inhumane. She agreed, but she said there was nothing she could do about that.

"Then why are you here?" I asked her.

"I need to hear your story. All of it. If I'm to defend you, I need to understand who you are and why you did what you did."

She stood in front of me. I was taller than her, as I was taller than everyone I had met since arriving on the planet. But I felt smaller. I felt my life had been diminished from what it had been, even though I don't remember anything of what it had been.

I recounted my long sad tale for her. She listened carefully, taking notes the entire time, and when I was finished, when I had explained how I had been shot more than once, and that when that happened I no longer wanted to live, and she offered her condolences.

"Thank you," I said.

"What do you want from my representation?"

"What can you do for me?"

"I can try to get you out of here. Let you enter greater society."

I nodded, but did not convey any indication as to whether I thought this was good or bad.

"Or I can make the circumstances here better for you. A more interesting mix of food and more of it. I can see to it that you get a nice apartment away from the other animals. You're half human so—"

"I get half the rights of other humans?"

"That's putting it a little crudely, but yes. You are not granted full rights, but you cannot be denied all rights."

"A legal conundrum."

"Yes," she said. "You will be a test case."

"How flattering."

"Don't be. It's usually not good to be a test case. Things can go very badly when lawyers embark on uncharted territory."

"Oh," I said.

"Exactly."

"I don't need to be away from the other animals."

"You don't?"

"They understand me."

She looked doubtful. I didn't blame her.

"I'm not saying we converse or anything like that," I said. "It's just that they see me for what I am."

"And what are you?" asked Mayel Johnson.

"I'm a creature that lives on the borders. All of them. Geographic, emotional, psychological, and, of course, physical."

"I thought they stayed away from you."

"They do. But they also understand me."

"I'm pledged to do what you want me to do," said Mayel.

"This case will make you famous," I said.

"That doesn't matter. You're a human being who needs a good defense."

"You're half right," I said.

"You don't need a good defense?"

"I'm not a human being. Only half one."

"Did you know that while you were tranquilized, they not only fixed your wounds, but they X-rayed you. They studied you. They were going to cut into you to find out more about your anatomy, but I put a stop to that as soon as I was assigned your case."

I blinked. I did not know any of those things. "Thank you," I said.

"You're welcome. But I didn't tell you that to elicit gratitude. I'm telling you so that you will understand what they want from you. They are not truly interested in prosecuting you. What they really want is to hold you captive. To study you."

I felt my hearts flutter. I had the sensation of being punched in the stomach. My legs went weak. I could hardly believe that a few words could turn me into a weakling, but there it was. That was exactly what happened.

"So I ask you once more," said Mayel. "I could see to it that you remain here. They would do their tests on you. Probably forever. For the rest of your life. And beyond. They would dissect you after you die. They would slice up your brain and delve into your innards. They would look for where you came from in the very substance of your flesh."

I shuddered.

"Or," said Mayel, "I could see to it that they never ever lay hands on you again without your express permission. I could have you declared a legal human being. In which case you would have all the rights and privileges of any other mortal human."

"You can really do that?"

"The precedents are there. The legal path is clear. I just have to take it."

"They'll oppose you."

"Of course, but they will lose. History bends toward justice. In your case justice is ensuring your freedom. Simple as that."

"I suspect nothing is simple in the law."

"Relatively simple, then."

"I see," I said.

"And you wouldn't have to wear those cuffs anymore."

"They think I can figure out how to escape," I said. "They keep my hands from being useful tools."

She nodded. "I know all that."

"Of course you do."

"I'm going to take what you've told me and prepare my case. Or, rather, prepare two cases. All I need is for you to tell me what you want. I'll come back in a couple of days."

I thanked her and then we said our good byes and I was alone with the other wild spirits.

I had a decision to make.

And I had no idea what it was going to be.

FORTY-SEVEN

That night the stars were bright pinpoints of light. They had always been that, but after my meeting with Mayel they felt even more so, as though someone had taken pins to the fabric of the sky and let the blinding light from the other side through. I had the feeling that those stars were there just for me, trying to let me know that the borderland known as the firmament understood my situation. My predicament.

Unable to sleep, I listened to night sounds. Howls of coyotes laced the air. There were dozens of them, it seemed. They would howl in unison, then fall into individual calls, like they each had a tune of their own.

I felt fear seep through me. The sound of carnivores in groups did something to my vegetarian equine half and I felt like prey, which did my psyche no good at all. If I was out in the world, would I always feel like prey? It was certainly possible.

I walked the grounds of the park. The grass was cold and wet. My breath clouded the air. I shivered. The fence around me was insurmountable. I could not jump over it and I could not open the gate. Even if it was unlocked, I could not undo the latch with my hands cuffed as they were.

But it also meant coyotes could not get inside. Neither could cougars, or bears, or any other creature that might find me tasty.

Most of the horses were tucked away in their stalls for the night, though there were a few of them out. They trotted away from me as I approached.

"I'm not evil," I said, not caring that they did not understand me.

I still felt some discomfort on my side, where the bullet had grazed me. They had done a fine job sewing me up. The scar was long and spectacular, like someone had tried to carve a channel into my skin.

The moon rose. It cast light on my surroundings, a silvery illumination that made everything look like it had been dusted with snow. It was a beautiful tableau, easing, for a moment, my discomfort with my hands being cuffed and the thought that I was to be an outcast for the rest of my life.

I trotted around the perimeter of the enclosure. It was a high fence of wire mesh, held in place with metal posts. I knew if I could harness the power of the horses and get them to work together, we could take down the fence. We could all have our freedom.

But they didn't particularly care about freedom, from what I could see. Probably didn't even have the concept. They just knew to graze and sleep.

I heard a voice behind me.

"Hey." A woman's voice. "Cal."

I turned around.

Lori, from the *ESCAPE!* program, was standing in the moonlight.

"You want out of here, or what?" she asked.

"I don't know," I said.

Silence for a split second. "Sure you do."

A guy holding a camera came up behind her. He trained the lens on me. A tiny red dot under the lens stared at me, unblinking. The gaze of millions of people channeled through it.

"Am I on the air now?" I asked.

"Of course."

"I haven't heard from you in a while."

"That doesn't matter. People want to know about you."

"What is there to know? I'm incarcerated."

"We can get you out."

"You'll go to jail."

"Wouldn't be the first time. We have smart lawyers. They get us out no matter what. We have the first amendment on our side."

I snorted, like a horse might. "Your show isn't about free expression."

"Shhh," she said. "Don't tell anyone." She grinned.

The shadows were playing tricks with the scene in front of me. She looked like she had black paint on her, as though someone was trying to make a portrait out of her image.

But that only took a minute proportion of my attention. What was taking the lion's share was that camera. It had a presence that I was finding more than a little irritating. I wanted only to have them turn it off. My life was not for public consumption. Not anymore.

"What's it like being an ex-candidate for president?" asked Lori.

"I am giving you fair warning," I said. "If you don't turn off that camera or point it to something else, I am going to smash it to bits."

"No you won't," said Lori. "You're much too interested in being famous. Everyone knows that. Wouldn't you say you were born to fame? I mean, given your physical make up?"

Some of the horses, roused by the noise, came trotting over. I wanted to put my hand on their necks and faces, assure them it was okay, but of course I couldn't.

The camera operator shifted from foot to foot. He was nervous. Lori was nervous, too, with all those horses converging on her. She hid it pretty well, though.

"Come on, Cal, tell us something interesting. Give us a *reason* for springing you. We aren't going to give you your freedom unless you tell us a real good story. Something that'll juice the ratings."

The camera operator stepped back.

"You want to help me?" I said.

"That's why we're here."

"I'll tell you what you want to know," I said, "if you cut my cuffs."

"We didn't bring anything to do that," said Lori. "But we will get you out. You know we can."

The horses, there were a good fifteen or so of them, had circled us and were staring us down as though they wanted to charge us. The tension was like a net over all of us.

That's when the drones moved in.

I heard the buzzing first and looked up. "What's that?" I asked, even though I knew exactly what it was.

"For our overhead shots," said Lori. "They've got infrared."

"Tell them to back off," I said.

She looked at me.

The horses began to stomp the ground. A herd mentality seemed to grab them and they began moving as one. They trotted to and fro. The camera operator dropped the camera. That startled the horses even more. They were seriously spooked. The drones came low. There were at least four of them.

"What the fuck?" I said, having to shout over the buzzing. "Why so many?"

"You're big news," said Lori. "We wanted to get all angles."

The camera operator was thoroughly frightened of the horse. He began running way.

"Al," said Lori, "come back here. Pick up your camera. Behave like a professional."

But Al wasn't interested in his job performance. He was only looking for an escape.

He ran between two horses, but they were scared of him and jostled him, then squeezed him between them.

He stumbled, fell to his knees, got up, took a few steps, then fell again.

The drones were less than ten feet above us. The horses began to run. They ran in circles around us, keeping in formation for the most part, but a few broke off from the herd and went rogue.

The camera operator, on the ground, covered his face with his hands and bent himself into a sea shell on the sand.

Horses ran over him. He screamed. They did not trample him.

Lori ran to the camera and picked it up and aimed it at the horses as they whizzed by. She kept up a voice over. "We're at the place of incarceration of Cal the centaur. Our drones seem to have caused a bit of a disturbance with the horses who are incarcerated with Cal. They are expressing their displeasure, as you can see."

The horses, now a thundering herd, ran away from us and the drones, across the field and toward the fence in the distance. The horses, I had to admit, were magnificent in the moonlight, frosted with snowy light, as though they had been dipped in silver flames. I watched them in awe as the infernal drones kept up their maddening buzzing sound as they hovered just out of my reach. I would have liked to grab each one and pull them down and trample them.

The camera operator took his chance and ran toward the fence near us, climbed it quickly, and cleared the top and went down the other side.

He stopped and looked at us.

"You'll never work again," said Lori. "I guarantee it."

He didn't seem to care. He turned from us and ran for all he was worth.

"He'll probably steal our van," said Lori.

"Shouldn't you go after him?"

She shrugged. "This is the story. Right here. You."

From off in the distance we heard the sound of crumpling metal. We both turned to look at the source.

The fence had been pushed down by the horses. They had made an escape route and were running through it, a river of motion under the moon.

I looked at Lori.

"We didn't do that," she said.

"You have wire cutters, don't you?"

She hesitated, which means she did. "No," she said.

"You came to rescue me, but you didn't bring anything to break the cuffs? I don't believe it."

The drones were a herd of their own and they seemed to want to drill their noise into my brain.

She glanced around. Not sure what she was looking for.

I advanced on her, feeling a little hostile, and a tiny bit enraged. Not enough to feel like I was going to lose control, but enough to make me think I had the capability of possibly hurting her.

When I felt that, I backed away from her.

She saw the trepidation in my face, I think. Or the frustration? Something, because then she reached into her back pocket, still holding the camera on me, and pulled out a pair of wire snips.

"We were going to use it to cut through the fence," she said.

"Now you can use it to cut the cuffs," I said.

She held the camera for a few more seconds. The drones gained a few feet of altitude, maybe to get a wider view of the scene. I wasn't sure.

Lori stepped toward me. I moved to the side, so she had access to my arms, but I was too tall for her to reach.

"I'll help you up," I said.

"I can't hold the camera and climb up at the same time," she said.

"You need to drop it," I said.

She bit her lip. "This is the best escape I've ever done. I can't lose the shot."

"Put it on the ground," I said.

She didn't want to.

"Do it!" I said.

She placed it so it was pointing up at me. I bent down on my front knees. She climbed up on my back and sat on my spine and I raised up on my front legs.

I felt the blades of the snips ease between my hands and she worked hard to press the blades against the links of the chain holding the cuffs in place.

"I'm working it," she said.

I felt a rush of adrenaline go through me as the cuffs broke loose.

They were still around my wrists, but my wrists were no longer bound together. I reached for the sky and pranced over the ground.

Freedom had its attractions, no doubt about it.

That's when I heard the sound of sirens, many of them, wailing hard, loud enough to begin to drown out the sound of the buzzing drones.

FORTY-EIGHT

I estimated the sirens were a couple of minutes away. The fence that the horses had broken down was less than thirty seconds away at a moderate gallop.

"You have two seconds to decide if you want to stay with me," I said to Lori.

She put her arms around my waist.

Headlights cut the dark air around us, beams shooting past us as the police cars headed over a rise and their flashing lights threw red and blue shadows all around us, illuminating the ground in alternating strobes.

I ran for all I was worth toward the break in the fence.

"You sure about this?" I called out to her.

"No!" she called back, her voice almost lost in the wind.

"Last chance," I said.

She moved closer, tightening her arms around my waist even harder, like she was afraid if she let me go, she would die.

Which, actually, was possible, since by then I was going at full speed, galloping over the ground with almost no thought to the hazards below me that my hooves might catch.

My wrists, still encumbered by the rings of the hand cuffs, felt weighty, the only artificial objects on me by then. I longed to have them gone, but knew that had to wait.

I put it out of my mind and instead concentrated on increasing my speed.

I approached the break in the fence at my fastest speed ever. My hooves cleared the air and I was flying at every stride, barely touching the ground as I went. Air whistled past my ears. I put my hands behind my back, between me and Lori, who barely moved to make room for them. I was reprising their configuration when I was cuffed, but I didn't care about that. I only wanted to streamline my form.

I jumped over the fallen fence. Lori tightened her grip even harder.

I entered the freedom of the wild with joy in my hearts, both of them.

I left the drones far behind.

The sirens also began to fade into the distance. No vehicle could follow me now. I was galloping over rocks and hills. I hit small pebbles as I ran that caused my hooves to skitter, but which didn't keep me from running hard.

My lungs were burning. I felt like my chest was being shredded from inside. I couldn't keep up this pace for long.

We were at least an hour or two from dawn, so the air was still dark. I ran harder and harder, but then Lori put her mouth near my ear and asked me to slow down.

"You're going to kill yourself," she said.

I was gasping for air, trying to pull the oxygen I needed from what seemed like the thinnest of reservoirs.

That's when I saw my ghost, floating in front of me, moving quickly, keeping pace with me. He was facing me, his horse head nodding and tossing. His human legs running backwards for all they were worth, lost in a blur of motion.

"Do you see that?" I asked Lori.

"See what?"

"In front of us. It's a reverse centaur."

After a pause I felt her shake her head side to side. "I don't see anything but the possibility you're going to run over something that'll break your legs in the dark."

I slowed my pace, then. The reverse centaur did the same.

I wasn't flying anymore, but running fast.

"I need water," I said.

"I don't have any," said Lori.

I slowed even more and stopped. My body was shaking, both aspects. My human half shivered in the cold. My horse half trembled.

Lori patted my back. "Better," she said.

My legs didn't want to stop. They tried to keep moving, shuffling and prancing and stepping here and there. The reverse centaur moved closer to me.

We were standing in an open field. Grassy clumps of vegetation everywhere, barely illuminated in the moonlight. No trees anywhere, just the flat field extending into the darkness.

The reverse centaur moved so close that I was able to reach out and touch it, which I tried to do, loosening my hands from behind me, and extending them with their wrist rings feeling like the worst symbol of freedom imaginable.

I stood with my hands outstretched for some time. Lori released her grip around me and leaned back on my equine spine. My breathing had relaxed a little. I was, at least, not within seconds of hyperventilating.

The reverse centaur regarded me for some time. Its eyes blinked and it reared its head a few times, as though I might have something to say to it and it was waiting for me.

I didn't. I actually, at that moment, yearned for his freedom, the freedom that comes from being nothing but a ghost.

Lori slid off my back to the ground. "Where are we?" she asked.

I didn't answer her. She pulled out her phone and tapped it. "No signal," she said. "Never thought I'd be somewhere my phone wouldn't work. Never wanted to be." She looked in the same direction I was looking. "What on Earth are you seeing out there?" she asked.

"My twin," I said.

"You've gone loopy," she said. "And taken me with you. Don't know what I was thinking, running with you."

"You were thinking that you might have an adventure if you stuck with me."

I was talking to her, but all my attention was on the reverse centaur.

Its eyes were big and black. They bulged out of their sockets. The eyelids looked impossibly inadequate to protecting them.

Lori patted my side, my equine side, where the long

scar had never truly healed over. It was still a ridge of tissue, marking one of my many wounds.

"You know," said Lori, "I think this was a mistake. I'm glad you got out, in principle. But it can't go well for you from here on out. They're going to track you down, and when they do, they'll keep you for good. Somewhere you won't be able to escape from. Even with our help."

I ignored her. The reverse centaur began drifting away from me. I followed, slowly.

"You listening to me?" asked Lori.

"No," I said.

She sighed. "I'm going to head back now. I won't tell any of them where you are. Not that I would know that anyway. Just to give you a little bit of time. A little taste of freedom. It won't be much. It'll be your last. But it'll be something."

She waited for me to say something.

I really had nothing to say. All of my answers seemed to be in the reverse centaur, standing in front of me.

"You know you burned bridges, right?" asked Lori.

The reverse centaur suddenly moved to one side and came close to Lori. She flinched and brushed at her shoulder. "What was that?" she asked.

"A friend," I said.

She kept brushing away—something. She didn't know what, but I could see that my reverse centaur was up to something. He wanted Lori to take action.

"I'm going to go find you water," she said.

"Good idea," I said.

The reverse centaur pulled away from Lori and me. He rose up off the ground and kept going higher. The drones returned then, all four of them. Somehow they had tracked me. Probably homing in on Lori, somehow. Following her heat signature?

Lori looked up. The drones hovered over us, but Lori kept walking away and the drones followed her. I heard their buzzing grow quieter as Lori moved away from me.

I didn't think she was going to find water for me. I didn't think she was truly interested in wanting to find water for me.

My reverse centaur had floated way up out of sight. It had given me the last key to my freedom. I no longer had drones following me. They were following Lori instead.

I turned away from Lori. I smelled something in the air. It was a scent I didn't quite recognize, not on a conscious level. And yet it seemed to call to me. It satisfied something deep inside me.

I followed the scent. It rose up out of the Earth. It seemed to wrap itself around the air surrounding me, and as I leaned into it, I suddenly knew what it was.

Water. The clear cool scent of flowing water, somewhere. I followed the smell for quite some time. Maybe a couple of miles. I was going slowly. My need to run had drained away from me. I was tired and it was all I could do to put one hoof in front of the other.

Before long I heard the sound of water flowing over

rocks, and I knew I was near a creek. The ground was going up. I climbed. The effort was a struggle.

As the first faint light of dawn barely lit the eastern horizon, I came to a bank of sand and gravel. I blinked and stepped forward. My hoofs touched cold water. It flowed around my ankles. I stood in the creek for a few seconds, then bent down and cupped my hands and drew up water and drank.

I was without anything, now. Just myself, my body, my mismatched, ad hoc, unreal body. No clothing, no home, no one.

Well, except for two objects that were not my property but were in my possession.

My cuff bracelets moved up and down my forearms as I repeatedly bent and lowered my human body to retrieve water and drink it. The cuffs, unlinked now, were a symbol of my freedom. I *was* free, but it was a provisional freedom. It depended on my ability to survive alone in an environment that promised predators and bad weather.

Once I had filled my horse belly with water and felt as refreshed as I was going to feel, I stepped away from the creek, gave silent thanks, and began to make my way to the mountains, just then taking on golden paint from the morning sun.

About the Author

Mario Milosevic's books include *Animal Life, Claypot Dreamstance, A Bestiary of Imaginary Species, Terrastina and Mazolli, The Last Giant, The Doctor and the Clown, 15 Strange Tales of Crime and Mystery,* and many others. He lives in Arizona with his wife, fellow writer Kim Antieau.

Bold, uncompromising, and guaranteed to enthrall, the new imprint from Green Snake Publishing features rich and compelling characters in pulse-pounding narratives that will keep you swiping left when you should be asleep. Immerse yourself in great storytelling and stay up all night with our addictive books. You might end up tired, but you won't be disappointed.

www.ingramcontent.com/pod-product-compliance
Lightning Source LLC
Chambersburg PA
CBHW031806200726
48289CB00014B/584